## Acclaim for Jessica Sorensen

### THE TEMPTATION OF LILA AND ETHAN

"Sorensen has true talent to capture your attention with each word written. She is creatively talented...Through the mist of demons that consume the characters' souls, she manages to find beauty in their broken lives." —TheCelebrityCafe.com

"A sweetly emotional read with two characters that just break your heart." —BadassBookReviews.com

"Perfect...This book was filled with everything that I've come to love from a Jessica Sorensen book...Loved it. I definitely recommend it." —BookBinge.com

"An emotional, romantic, and really great contemporary romance... Lila and Ethan's story is emotionally raw, devastating, and heart-wrenching." —AlwaysYAatHeart.com

"Sorensen has me pining for my next hit every time I finish one of her books. I devoured this and am now feeling some withdrawals. It's like a drug. You want more and more and more." —UndertheCvoersBookBlog.com

### THE FOREVER OF ELLA AND MICHA

"Breathtaking, bittersweet, and intense...Fans of *Beautiful Disaster* will love the series." —CaffeinatedBookReviewer.com

"Powerful, sexy, emotional, and with a great message, this series is one of the best stories I've read so far."

—BookishTemptations.com

"Another touching and emotional read that will leave you on the verge of tears at times and make your heart soar at others."

—BadassBookReviews.com

"A fun, sexy, unforgettable story of first love…will blow you away."

—UndertheCoversBookBlog.com

## THE SECRET OF ELLA AND MICHA

"Sorensen's portrayal of…relationships and long-distance love, as well as the longing to escape one's past, raises her above her new adult peers."

—*RT Book Reviews*

"A fantastic story…very addictive…This book will hook you in and you will feel hot, steamy, and on the edge of your seat.

—Dark-Readers.com

"A beautiful love story…complicated yet gorgeous characters…I am excited to read more of her books."

—SerendipityReviews.co.uk

"Fantastic…a great read…I couldn't put this book down…I was sad when it came to an end."

—TheBookScoop.com

"A really great love story. There is something epic about it…If you haven't jumped on this New Adult bandwagon, then you need to get with the program. I can see every bit of why this story has swept the nation."

—TheSweetBookShelf.com

"Absolutely loved it…This story broke my heart…I can't wait to get my hands on the next installment."

—Maryinhb.blogspot.com

"Wonderful…delightful…a powerful story of love…will make your heart swoon."

—BookswithBite.net

## THE REDEMPTION OF CALLIE & KAYDEN

"Enjoyable, moving…a beautifully written story."

—JacquelinesReads.blogspot.com

"The author did an amazing job of having the reader connect to the characters and feel for them as you read…I want *more*!"

—JessicasBookReview.com

"Extremely emotional and touching…It made me want to cry, and jump for joy."

—Blkosiner.blogspot.com

"I couldn't put it down. This was just as dark, beautiful, and compelling as the first [book]…Nothing short of amazing…Never have I read such emotional characters where everything that has happened to them seems so real."

—OhMyShelves.com

"[It] draws on human emotions and takes you into dark places. Although brimming with angst, it's a love story that will overflow your heart with hope. This series is not to be missed."

—UndertheCoversBookblog.com

### THE COINCIDENCE OF CALLIE & KAYDEN

"Another great story of passion, love, hope, and themes of salvation."

—BookishTemptations.com

"Romantic, suspenseful, and well written—this is a story you won't want to put down."

—*RT Book Reviews*

"An emotional rollercoaster."

—TotalBookaholic.com

# Take Chances:
# Three Stories

# Take Chances: Three Stories

## JESSICA SORENSEN

New York Boston

Copyright © 2014 by Jessica Sorensen
Excerpt from *The Secret of Ella and Micha* copyright © 2012 by Jessica Sorensen
Excerpt from *Breaking Nova* copyright © 2013 by Jessica Sorensen
Cover design by Brigid Pearson
Cover photograph by Regina Wamba
Cover copyright © 2014 by Hachette Book Group, Inc.

Forever Yours
Hachette Book Group
237 Park Avenue, New York, NY 10017
HachetteBookGroup.com
Twitter.com/foreverromance

First ebook and print on demand edition: July 2014

Forever Yours is an imprint of Grand Central Publishing.
The Forever Yours name and logo are trademarks of Hachette Book Group, Inc.

The publisher is not responsible for websites (or their content) that are not owned by the publisher.

The Hachette Speakers Bureau provides a wide range of authors for speaking events. To find out more, go to www.hachettespeakersbureau.com or call (866) 376-6591.

ISBN 978-1-4555-8522-9 (ebook)
ISBN 978-1-4555-8523-6 (print on demand)

*This one's for all my readers.*
*Thanks for all your support!*

# Acknowledgments

A huge thanks to my family for supporting me and my dream. You guys are awesome!

And an extra thanks to my agent, Erica Silverman, and my editor, Amy Pierpont, for all your help and input.

And to everyone who reads this book, an endless amount of thank-yous.

# Contents

*Lila and Ethan:*
*Forever and Always*

# *Chapter 1*

## Lila

There are four things I've learned about the outdoors over the last month since Ethan and I first began our cross-country road trip: (1) It always feels cold living outdoors, even when it's July and we're in Virginia; (2) the mountains seem to breed pine needles and dirt; (3) the camping food (heavy sigh)... I'm not even sure what to say about it. Pop-Tarts and fruit snacks that don't even taste like fruit. Beans in a can—gross. And s'mores; they're nothing but burnt marshmallows, crackers, and messy chocolate that makes me wish I was eating the delicious s'mores cake made by Delina's Bakery and Simple Cakes that was on the corner of the street I grew up on. The chocolate there was divine.

There is one thing, though, that I can certainly admit is a plus about being outdoors—and it's the fourth thing I've learned during this trip and the one thing that I'll miss when we head back to Vegas tomorrow—the beauty of the night sky. Nothing I've ever seen before can compare to it. It's so open and full of stars and the moon is so bluntly bright, way more than in the city, since there are no city lights to outshine it. It's simplistically beautiful. Plus Ethan loves looking at the stars and being with him while he lies on the ground and stares up at them makes me love the sight even more... Okay, so maybe I've learned five things and have one more thing that I'll miss: (5) Being with Ethan all the time—as long as Ethan's with me, I'm fine with being cold, getting covered in pine needles, and eating beans straight from a can. I could do all those things with him forever.

I just wish I knew that he felt the same way. But I don't know what he thinks about our future because he doesn't like talking about it and it makes me sad and bummed out whenever I think about the unknown that lies before me. About him and I and where we'll end up.

"What are you thinking about?" Ethan asks as he holds a stick with a marshmallow attached to the end of it, heating it just above the fire. It's his third one and it seems like he's never going to stop, like he's never going to get enough of getting his fingers sticky.

"How gross melted marshmallows are," I tell him the partial truth, relaxing back on my hands. I'm sitting on a log and my hair hasn't been washed in days. There's a tent behind me, a cooler to the side of me, and campfire in front of me, blowing smoke in my face. And when I rub my thumb across my forearm, a layer of black comes off. Not one of my finest moments, but with the way Ethan's looking at me—with want and love in his eyes—it makes me feel very attractive, even in a hoodie and dirt-stained jeans.

Ethan cocks a dark eyebrow at me, his black hair falling into his eyes as he leans down to pick up a piece of wood by his feet and toss it into the fire. "Only you would be thinking that," he says over the crackle of the flames as he stretches his legs out and relaxes back against the cooler. He continues to roast the marshmallow in the fire, the outer part turning black and smoking. I don't say anything about him burning it, because I know that's how he likes them. Instead I just watch him, feeling myself warm inside like the melted goo on the end of his stick as he chews on his lip and observes the flames.

He's so sexy, even when he hasn't showered in days. The unshaven face, torn jeans, and wrinkled black T-shirt work so well on him. Plus his tattoos...God he's so gorgeous, all grungy and manly. I could practically have an orgasm just looking at him.

Suddenly he smirks at me, totally busting me for checking him out, and I blink my gaze off him and focus back on the conversation.

"What do you mean only I would think that?" I ask, tucking a strand of my chin-length blond and black hair behind my ear. "Lots of people don't like melted marshmallows."

"Not true. A lot of people like them," he says, rotating the stick in his hand. "You just have weird taste in food." A teasing look rises on his face as he grins. "Or maybe I should just say bad taste in food."

Scowling, I reach over to the bag of marshmallows between us, pick one up, and throw it at him. It's dark enough that he has a hard time seeing me and it ends up pegging him in the forehead. I laugh as I dust the dirt off my hands and sit up straight, feeling a little bit better.

"You're going to pay for that one," Ethan warns, and through the glow of the fire, his eyes look as black as the smoldering wood. He removes the stick from the flames as he gets to his feet. After blowing on it a few times, he carefully plucks the marshmallow from the end of the stick and mushes it between his fingers. At first I think he's going to eat it, but instead he winds around the fire pit between us, heading toward me.

"Don't even think about it." I start to get to my feet but by the time I stand up, he's within arm's reach. I stumble back, shaking my head. "Don't," I plead as he stretches his hand out toward me, the gooey marshmallow all over his fingers inching closer to my face. "Please, I don't want to get sticky."

"I think you need to get sticky." He takes another step toward me and I match his movement, stepping back, my heels bumping against a log on the ground.

"Ethan, I swear to God, please don't," I plead with my hands out in front of me. "They taste so gross and my mouth will feel gross for the rest of the night."

He sighs, lowering his hand to his side. "I won't just as long as you tell me what you were really thinking about earlier," he says. I open my mouth to lie to him again, but he holds up his hand. "And don't tell me marshmallows, because I know that's not true. You had that look on your face, the one you get when you're thinking about something that upsets you."

I frown at the fact that he can read me that well and I don't want to tell him what I was thinking about. How I'm worried about our future because I have no idea what's going to happen today, tomorrow, whether we'll be together or whether he even wants to be with me in the future since he refuses to talk about it. I know he loves me and sometimes I think he can't even help it. Ethan's never been one for planning much of anything and I think talking about our future means he'd be planning for the future. I also think he might be scared of what we might become if we did commit—what would happen to our relationship.

"You've been so mopey ever since Chicago," he adds through my silence.

My frown deepens. He's right. I have been really mopey ever since we visited Ella and Micha in Chicago. Micha had been there for a few days playing at a concert. Seeing Ella and Micha again made me start really wondering about my future with Ethan.

It was Ella and Micha's six-month anniversary as husband and wife and they seemed so happy. It makes me sad, because even though I'm happy with my relationship with Ethan, I want to be his forever, and Ethan has already made it pretty clear how he feels about weddings and marriage and all that "ridiculous nonsense" (his words not mine).

It's not like I want to get married today or even in a year because I don't. I'm not ready for that yet, *but* I want to know that five or ten years down the road we could be standing up in front of a minister, saying our "I dos." That we could end up having what Ella and Micha have.

"Just tell me what's bothering you," he interrupts my thoughts with a fake sexy pout. "Or else I'm going to have to stuff this marshmallow in your mouth and then you're going to be grumpy because you'll be all sticky."

I narrow my eyes with my hands on my hips. "You wouldn't dare."

"You don't think so?" he questions, elevating his eyebrows.

I sigh, knowing he would do it in a heartbeat and laugh at me. But it's part of why I love him, because in the end I'd laugh too. "Fine," I say, searching for a way around this without telling the truth to avoid him getting uncomfortable and weird like he always does whenever anyone starts talking about life and the future. "I'm mopey because we've been in the mountains for too long and I need a shower."

He studies me intently with his head cocked to the side. I think he's buying it until suddenly his tattooed arm springs forward and he stuffs melted marshmallow into my mouth.

"Dammit, Ethan!" I shout, my voice muffled by the goo. I lick my lips and wipe them with the back of my hand, trying to get rid of the stickiness while Ethan grins at me, completely proud of himself.

"That's a good look for you," he says, brushing his fingers along my bottom lip and wiping off some of the goo. He licks his fingers and I pull a face because I really do hate melted marshmallows. "Tastes good too," he mutters, his humor shifting to desire as he eyes my lips. Then suddenly he's cupping the back of my head and drawing me in for a kiss. The moment his lips crash into mine, I forget what we were talking about or even that we're in the mountains. I just kiss him back, willingly parting my lips to let his wet tongue slide into my sticky mouth.

"Really good," he whispers against my mouth, and then kisses me again, his fingers threading through my hair and pulling gently at the roots, making my skin tingle.

My fingers wander up his back, my hands trembling with the abundance of emotions I feel for him. Want. Desire. Need. It's so terrifying. Knowing how bad I want this. Want him. And that one day maybe it could be all gone.

In almost a desperate move, I pull him closer to me, clinging on to him, the heat of his body warming up the chilly breeze of the mountains. It also warms up my heart, makes me feel the slightest bit better and content, and reminds me that despite the fact that I might never get married—that I have no idea where we're headed—having moments like these with Ethan is completely and utterly worth drifting into the unknown.

I just wish it could be different.

\* \* \*

# Ethan

We've been on the road for almost a month now, living off of the money we saved up after five months of working—me in construction and working part-time as a bartender, and Lila waitressing and working at a clothing store on the weekends. We were supposed to go earlier but it took longer to save up than I'd planned. But we busted our asses off, saving everything we could so we could live on the road for a month straight. It's been amazing—every day is with Lila. The only thing that sucks is that we're heading back to Vegas tomorrow, back to life and the real world, popping the secluded, quiet bubble we've built around us during our road trip.

Still, I'm trying to make the best of our last night here, especially because she seems sort of down and I hate seeing her down. It worries me a little, since in the past she used pills as a way not to feel her sadness. She was addicted to them for a very long time and I was the one who helped her with the addiction, watched her struggle with it, but conquer it. She's had such a hard life and I want her to be happy all the time, even though that's impossible... I wish I could find a way to make it possible.

After I push the marshmallow into Lila's mouth, I feel her mood lighten, which was what I was trying to accomplish. But my playfulness quickly turns to desire as she tries to lick the goo off her lips. I want to taste it—taste her—so I kiss her fiercely while I start to back us toward the tent. My hands travel up the back of her shirt and I savor the softness of her skin as I try to find the zipper to the door of the tent with my other hand. I manage to get the tent unzipped without disconnecting our lips; then I guide her inside and down onto her back onto the sleeping bags before covering her body with mine. I kiss her until she becomes breathless, until she's clutching my arms so tightly her fingernails are scraping my skin and she begs me to be inside her.

I nearly lose it right there. She's too beautiful for her own good and it makes lasting long nearly impossible. "Fuck, Lila, you're going to make this end quickly if you keep saying stuff like that," I say, pulling away to remove her jacket. She eagerly helps me, slipping her arms out of the sleeves. Then I tug her shirt off and unhook her bra, laughing when she gets the strap tangled up and stuck on her arm. Finally after a lot of laughing, I get it off and toss it aside, then lower my lips back to hers and slip my tongue deep inside her mouth, which tastes like marshmallow.

"Ethan…" She groans, lacing her fingers through my hair as she curves her back, pressing her chest against mine.

I grip her hip with one hand, pulling her closer to me until there's no room left between us. Then my fingers slide up her side as I devour the taste of her. When I reach her breast, I graze my finger across her nipple and she gasps in response, her legs fastening around me. Our tongues tangle and our breaths mix as she grinds her hips against mine and rubs up against me. I move with her, listening to her moan and gasp and plead until I can't take it anymore. I lean back and yank my shirt off, throwing it to the side of the tent. Then I undo the button on her jeans and she impatiently helps me as I slip them down her legs. When I get to her ankles, she kicks off the jeans and strips off her panties. Then she reaches to pull me to her, but I shake my head and hold on to her ankle.

"What's wrong?" she says, practically panting.

I don't respond as I kiss a path up the inside of her leg all the way to her thigh, breathing her in with each touch of my mouth. I pause at the top, looking down at her as she stares up at me, her eyes wide and full of want. It's dark, but the glow of the moon and the fire outside glimmers in through the screen and open door on the tent. She's beautiful, flawless skin, full lips, wide, glittering eyes, and her breathing is ravenous, revealing how nervous she is and how much she trusts me to be with her like this, touching her in a way no one else has, because I love her.

I trace my fingers across her collarbone and she sighs, her eyelids fluttering shut. "I want you inside me," she whispers, her back arching against my touch. "Please, Ethan...I can't take it anymore."

I smile as I slowly lower my mouth to her breast. "I want to touch you everywhere...God, I want you...," I breathe against her skin, savoring the moment before taking her nipple into my mouth. She moans, her breath hitching, and her fingers find my hair again as I suck a little bit harder.

Both of us are sweaty and gasping and finally my mouth leaves her nipple just so I can breathe. I want more, though. Need fucking more. So I make a path of kisses down her stomach, sucking on her skin. When I reach her thighs, I spread them and she grasps on to me as I dip my face between her legs and slide my tongue deep inside her. My eyes slip shut...my fingers tightening around her thighs...God, the taste of her never gets old—never will. None of this will.

I continue to taste her while her hips writhe against my mouth, until I feel like I'm going to explode; then I pull away and kiss my way up her stomach and chest to her mouth. Her lips part as I slide my tongue in for a kiss that makes both of us groan. I work to get the button of my jeans undone as she grips my arms, holding me to her, kissing me fervently. I only pull away to take my jeans and boxers off. Then I get a condom out of my wallet, put it on, and situate back between her legs.

With one hard thrust, I'm sliding deep inside her. Our lips

connect somewhere in the middle and I grip her thigh, bending one of her legs up to my side as I rock into her. She rhythmically moves with me, our skin dampening with sweat, until we become lost in each other over and over again. Eventually we cry out together as I give one final thrust inside her, then we lose ourselves completely.

Afterward, I lie still inside her with my head on her chest, feeling her pulse race as she rests against the sleeping bags, running her fingers through my hair. "You have the softest hair," she whispers with an exhausted sigh.

I push up from her and look her in the eyes. "Is that supposed to be a compliment? Because I'm not sure if a guy's hair should be soft," I tease.

She continues to rub her fingers through my hair. "Yeah, it should be. And yours is the softest."

I chuckle under my breath and then return my head back onto her chest. It gets really quiet as she continues to run her fingers through my hair. I listen to the fire crackling outside, the sound of an owl in the distance, and the river flowing through the trees.

"God, it sucks that we have to head home tomorrow," I say, letting out a loud breath.

"I know you're sad," she says. "And I'm sort of sad that we won't be spending as much time together, but at the same time I'm really, really excited about taking a real shower."

I smile, shaking my head. "Not me. If I could, I'd keep doing this forever." I yawn, feeling exhaustion take me over. "Although, I'll admit. I do sort of get sick of driving. I'd love to take a break from that."

"You will," she says. "As soon as we get home, we can go on a driving strike."

"Yeah, that sounds nice, but it'll have to be after I go back home for my mom's birthday in August."

Her hand stops moving through my hair. "You're going back to Star Grove in August?"

I glance up at her. "Yeah...didn't I tell you?"

I can't read her expression, but she seems tense. "No, you never mentioned it."

Shit. I think I might've messed up on that one. "I'm sorry," I say. "I thought I told you about it a while ago."

She shakes her head, not looking at me but up at the tent roof. "Well, you didn't." She pauses, and I can feel that she's struggling to breathe. "So you're going in August?"

"Yeah..." I'm not sure what to do to make her feel better. I didn't mean to not tell her. Sometimes I just sort of fuck up, forgetting that I can't just do things based upon what I want—that I'm in a relationship now. "I'm only going to be gone for a few days. I promise."

"Okay." It's all she says, which makes the situation way worse, because she's obviously bothered by this. But I wonder if it's just because I didn't tell her about it or because I'm going alone. Or maybe it's something else entirely—she's been upset a lot lately. "Lila, I can tell something's bugging you, so will you please just talk to me?" I skim my finger across her cheekbone, causing her to shudder. "You seem upset and if you'd just tell me why, maybe I could help."

"I'm fine...I promise." She closes her eyes and inhales deeply and I think she's on the verge of crying.

"I wish you'd just talk to me more about stuff," I say quietly, not just hoping she'll tell me what's bothering her now but hoping she'll finally break and spill what's been putting her in a downer mood for the last couple of weeks as well. "You usually do."

But she stays silent and I let her play with my hair for a few more moments before I carefully slip out of her and roll onto my back. She follows me, hitching her leg over my stomach; then she traces a circular pattern across my sweaty chest.

"I'm sorry I've been so cranky," she whispers in a choked voice. "My head's just been in a really weird place. And I don't care if you go see your mom on her birthday—you should."

"It's okay to be cranky sometimes," I reply, wrapping my arm around her and pulling her closer to me. "But you should really just talk to me and let me help make you feel better. No matter what's bugging you, I'm here for you."

She shakes her head and nuzzles her face against my chest. "I don't want to talk about it tonight, but maybe tomorrow." She sounds so sad and it hurts, not knowing what's causing it. If it's something because of me.

Whatever's bothering her—and has been bothering her—she doesn't want to tell me, and even though Lila has opened up to me about a lot of things, I still know from past experience that she can keep a secret like no one else. All those years of popping pills and no one ever knew.

Minutes later she falls asleep in my arms and I stroke my finger up and down her back, listening to the quiet around us that only being in the mountains can bring, attempting to sort through my thoughts.

She's been really up and down since Chicago, ever since we went to visit Ella and Micha a couple of weeks ago. I'm not exactly sure why, but I think it might have to do with the fact that she wants to get married, something that was brought up during Ella and Micha's wedding last Christmas. Yeah, I knew Lila had certain things she wanted out of life, but I hadn't really thought she'd need to say "I do" one day, until she started rambling about it while she was helping Ella plan things for the wedding. For a week straight, it's all I heard about—that and babies, since Ella's sister-in-law was pregnant. I tried to shrug and nod whenever she brought it up, and it seemed to be working for me, until she flat out asked me for a response.

"Where do you see us in five years?" she'd asked while we were tying bows at Micha's mom's kitchen table.

I'd glanced up from the bow I was tying, a little startled by her question. "Huh?"

Lila peered up at me with her beautiful blue eyes. "You and I as a couple. Do you think we'll still be together in five years?"

"I'm not sure…" I'd squirmed uncomfortably in the chair. "I mean, we've only been dating for like a month."

"Dating, yeah," she said. "But we've been friends for longer and Ella and Micha were friends first, which makes the fact that they're getting married so young understandable, at least from my point of view."

I finished tying the bow before I spoke again, deciding just to be honest with her. "Honestly, Lila, I don't think I can ever see myself getting married… if that's what you're getting at." I wasn't sure it was. She was utterly confusing me.

She shrugged, reaching for a roll of ribbon. "I wasn't getting at anything. Just wondering, since you seem so against marriage." She swallowed hard, looking upset. "Glad to know where you stand."

I sighed as she pushed her chair away from the table and got to her feet. "Lila, I—"

She'd held up her hand, silencing me. "I wasn't expecting a proposal anytime in the near future, but the fact that you can never see yourself getting married sucks." Then she'd left the room and I felt like the biggest asshole.

Still do.

But I can't help how I feel. Or how I think I feel. I'm honestly unsure of what I want or how I can figure it out, since I hate figuring heavy stuff out. I don't like complications and weddings and marriage, and forevers are more than complicated, at least from what I've seen. My parents' marriage was full of fighting and abuse and that's the last thing I want. Plus, making things really complicated means there's a chance they could fall apart and then I'd be left dealing with the outcome. I had a girlfriend, London, who I thought I loved—although now that I'm in love with Lila, I'm not so sure I was really in love with London—and then she fell out a window and got amnesia and everything I had with her was lost. It was really hard to get over. If something like that happened with Lila and me…if I lost her in any way…I'm not sure I could ever get over it.

There are so many reasons why marriage and a future scare the shit out of me and I don't think can't picture myself doing it. I really can't.

Lila eventually let the marriage thing go, obviously, since she's here with me seven months later, but I can tell whenever the future comes up that she's waiting for me to tell her what I want, but I still don't have an answer to give her. I want her. That much I know. She's amazing and smart and brave. She's more beautiful than she realizes and even though I hate to admit it, I love giving in to her and letting her have her way…most of the time anyway.

But I've planned on living my life carefree and doing whatever I want, whenever I feel like it, like I am now without worrying about other stuff. And if five years down the road, I want to get up one day and take off in my truck and just drive off into the unknown by myself, I still want to be able to do it without hurting anyone or worrying about what will happen to those around me—worrying about life. That I might be breaking someone. Or that I won't be able to because of my own feelings and attachments to certain things. But if I'm married, then that means I'll have a wife to think about, a steady job, a house, and one day maybe even kids. God…I'm not sure how I feel about that.

The only thing I am sure about is that I never, ever want to lose Lila. She's the only girl who's ever made me feel like a relationship is worth the risk. And she's not even just my girlfriend. She's my best friend. The only person I've ever felt comfortable enough with to talk openly to. I tell her as much personal stuff as I tell my journal. But if we don't want the same things, I'm not sure how long I'll be able to hold on to her.

# Chapter 2

## Lila

It's our last day here—on the road together—and I'm both sad for it to end and kind of glad to be going back so I can take a real shower and eat food that doesn't come in a can. I'm trying to keep as upbeat as I can even after my little meltdown last night. I didn't really mean to almost cry last night in the tent, but then he started talking about how he was going up to Star Grove for his mom's birthday. He never told me he was, which stung a little. But the worst part is that he didn't even invite me to go with him. I don't think he's doing it on purpose. I just think that he's not really thinking about the future as an *us* yet. It painfully reminded me even more that I have no idea where we're going to end up—if I'll ever visit his parents' with him. And what added more heartache to the situation was having him near me, touching me like he does. It sets off how much I want things to always be this way.

Forever and always. Just him and I.

I just wish he felt the same way, but I'm starting to wonder more and more if he doesn't.

Still, I pull myself together and manage to make it through breakfast smiling. The only time I let my mood drop is when it's time to get cleaned up, but that's for an entirely different reason. No matter what section of the country we're in, all places share one thing in common. The streams and ponds are freezing. Taking a bath outside and actually staying in long enough to get clean is a challenge. It takes a lot of mental preparation. As I strip off my clothing and stare at the translucent water rolling over the rocks in front of me, I shiver, even though the sun is beating down my bare body.

It's an amazing sight, really. The small pond is tucked between rocks and trees, the water a clear blue, and there's this little waterfall toward the back. But I know from experience that the beauty of it is going to be lost the moment I step in and I start to freeze.

"You know, you were sexy as hell before," Ethan says from behind me. "But that tattoo makes you look so goddamn gorgeous."

I smile to myself, remembering how I'd finally decided to get a tattoo right before we left for this road trip. It took me a while to figure out what I wanted, but then decided on a sparrow when I found out it meant freedom. It seems fitting since I've never felt freer in my life. Per Ethan's suggestion, I got it right between my shoulder blades. It hurt, but it was totally worth it because with each prick of the needle, I felt freer and freer from my dark past and my parents' control.

*I am free now.*

"You know, if you want, you can just stand there all day," Ethan adds, and I can hear the soft sound of his footsteps inching closer to me. "You make the view a hell of a lot better."

I look over my shoulder at him, giving him a dark, playful look.

"What if some hikers came up here and saw me naked? Would you still want me to stand here naked?"

He's standing not too far off behind me near the tree line, wearing a dark green shirt with a faded logo, cargo shorts, and boots that are untied. He's also got his journal in his hands. "That depends," he says, taking a step forward, his intent gaze making me feel like I'm sweltering.

"On what?" I'm breathless just from the way he's looking at me.

He cocks his head to the side, a grin gradually rising on his face as he leisurely scrolls over my body. "On if the hikers are guys or women. If it's a bunch of women, then I'd tell them to go ahead and enjoy the view." His grin broadens as I roll my eyes.

"You're such a pervert," I say, crossing my hands over my chest.

He reaches me, assessing me, and the desire in his eyes makes me shiver. "You like that I am—it totally turns you on when I say dirty things to you."

"It does not," I lie, biting back a smile.

He arches his brow. "If that's not true, then why are your nipples all perky?" He reaches out and pinches one of them softly, causing me to shudder, and a small gasp escapes my lips.

"You want to get in with me?" I ask as he cups my breast and leans in to suck on my neck. *Please, get in with me. Oh my God, please…*

He kisses me until I become breathless and then moves back with a glazed look in his eyes. "Maybe in a bit." He's totally enjoying the fact that he's making me all hot and bothered. "I'm just going to watch you while I write for a while."

I frown, a little disappointed as I back toward the water. "You're such a tease."

Pleased with himself, he heads over to one of the large rocks next to the stream that pools into the pond and climbs up on it. When he gets to the top, he sits down and situates the journal on his lap. Then he takes a pen out of his pocket, bites off the cap, and presses the tip of it to the paper as he watches me with an *I'm waiting for you to get into the water so I can watch you wet and naked* look.

Sighing, I approach the edge of the stream, where the water meets the dirt. Mud oozes through my toes and rocks scrape at my bare feet as I dip my toe into the water. My body instantly jolts from the chill as I take a deep breath and wade in, squealing and sucking in huge lungfuls of air. When I reach the middle, where the water goes up to my waist, I turn around and find Ethan laughing at me.

"A little cold?" he asks through his laughter.

I shake my head, then decide the best way to get even is to torture him, so even though it's not comfortable to do in cold water, I dip my head back into the water, arch my back, and stick my chest up in the air. As the water soaks my hair, it gives me a brain freeze, like I've just guzzled down an ICEE, but it's worth it when I stand back up to see Ethan looks a little flustered.

I smile to myself and then turn around and plunge under, letting the water wash over my body, so cold not a single bad thought can form in my head. Moments later, I hear a soft thud from behind me. When I turn around, Ethan has hopped off the rock and is peeling off his shirt. Without taking his shorts off, he walks into the water, wincing from the cold as it reaches his waist.

"What are you doing?" I ask as he wades toward me. "I thought you were just going to watch and write for a while."

He doesn't speak, just shakes his head. His eyes are locked on mine and full of desire as he moves toward me. When he reaches me, he gives no warning, crashing his lips against mine and scooping me up in his arms. The sun hits my skin as I'm picked up out of the water and my legs fasten around his waist. He holds onto me with one hand as he feels my side and skims my breast with his other hand, kissing me until I can't breathe. I clutch him as his fingers drift from my side, to my hip, to my thigh. Then bracing me in one arm, he slips a finger deep inside me.

I gasp as I tangle my fingers through his hair and desperately try to grasp on to him. One of my legs slides back down into the water and I stand on my tiptoes, clutching onto his shoulders, with my other leg hitched around his hip. His fingers move inside me, driving me to the edge as he buries his head into the crook of my neck, his warm breath caressing my chilly skin. I groan. I plead. I beg for more and he gives it to me, slipping another finger into me, and I move my hips with his rhythm until he pushes me over the edge. I forget about everything. Nothing exists at this moment except for him and I and the connection we've shared since the moment we met over two years ago.

It's perfect until he pulls his fingers out of me and leans back a little, letting my other leg slide down back into the water. Then I just feel cold again.

"I couldn't resist," he says, tucking a strand of my wet hair behind my ear. "You looked too tempting not to touch…God, I have such a hard time keeping my hands off you."

"But what about you?" I say, putting my hand on his lean chest.

"You can pay me back later," he says with a wink and a grin.

I smile and then he kisses me before backing away to the shore, his shorts soaking wet and hanging at his hips. Beads of water drip down his chest and tattooed side as he makes his way back to the rocks, smiling at me like he's so happy. Just like I should be. And I am. But every perfect moment could be our last one together and that makes me sad.

After he climbs back up on the rocks, I start scrubbing my body down with water, while Ethan starts to write. I finish up quickly, then wade back to the shore and out of the water. The frigid air hits my body like a wall of snow and I scurry for the towel I hung up on a tree branch. I wrap it around me and wring my hair out before heading over to Ethan. He still has his shirt off, his wet shorts drying in the sunlight peeking through the tree branches above him. He's got his head tipped down, his black hair falling into his eyes as he jots down words, losing touch with reality like he always does whenever he writes. I climb onto the rock beside him and sit down next to him, leaning over my shoulder to get a peek at what he's writing, even though he never wants me to see.

"What are you writing about today?" I ask, and he jumps, like he didn't even realize I was up here.

He hurries to finish what he's writing and closes the journal. "Nothing important," he says. "I was just thinking about stuff.... About going back home...returning to the city and life..." He gazes out at the pine trees to the side of us, looking really sad and lost. "We should probably get going if we want to make it back and have a little time to relax before we go back to normal life."

"Are you sure you want to go back?" I ask, leaning back to look him in the eyes. "You seem so sad about it."

He shrugs and when he meets my gaze, I can see his sadness deepen. "We kind of have to, don't we?"

"Unless we want to lose our jobs," I reply sadly, because even though I can't wait to get back and take a real shower, I'll also really miss my time alone with him. "I mean, Denny was understanding and everything, but he's going to flip if I call him up and ask him for more time off." I actually lucked out with Denny, my boss at this restaurant where I waitress. When I told him my plans for this road trip, he understood and said something about only being young once. He's having his niece fill in for me while I'm gone and promised me I'd still have my job when I get back, but I doubt that'd be the case if I stayed away too much longer.

"Yeah, I'm supposed to start work on that house being built up on Maple Street in a week." He sighs heavy heartedly. "I guess it's time to return to the real world." He pauses, assessing me. "Although…" He trails off, cracking the tiniest smile.

"What?" I ask as he stares at me with this strange look on his face. "Why are you looking at me like that?"

He shrugs, his smile expanding. "Because I was thinking about taking another route back home."

"What sort of route?" I ask curiously.

He bites on the end of his pen, studying me, his eyes following the beads of water rivering from my hair down my chest. "I was thinking maybe the beach sort of route."

My mood perks up and it seems to boost his too. "Are you being serious? You want to stop by the beach on our way home?"

He nods, his smile breaking all the way through. "Yeah… you've been saying how much you hate the cold and so I figured we could head down south to South Carolina and spend a day there before we head west… maybe to the beach you said you went to as a kid."

I attempt not to smile, but I can't help it. "I can't believe you remembered that."

He sets his journal aside and scoots closer to me. "How could I not?" he asks, cupping my cheek. "It was probably the only pleasant story you've ever told me about your childhood."

"That's because I went on the vacation with my friend's family," I tell him. "Not my own family."

"I remember," he says. "You said it was your favorite vacation ever."

"It was… I actually felt happy for once… and content." I pause. "Although, this one easily tops it."

He gives me a questioning look. "I'm kind of surprised you said that."

I'm baffled. "Why? I've been having fun and I thought you knew that."

"I did know, but…" He struggles, shifting his weight, and then he places his hands on the tops of my thighs. "You've been so upset since Chicago…and then last night…" He waits for me to explain, but I still don't feel like I want to tell him.

"It's not because of the vacation," I promise. "Although I'm not a huge fan of the mountains, I'm still having fun with you… everything is fun with you."

"Then why does it seem like you've been upset lately?" he asks, searching my eyes for something. "Ever since we visited Ella and Micha. And you won't talk about it."

"Ethan…" I trail off, unsure. "I just don't think I can talk to you about this."

"Why not?" he asks, starting to get frustrated. "Goddammit, Lila. I wish you'd just tell me because it's driving me crazy. You tell me a lot of things and now suddenly you won't…it makes me think it has something to do with me."

I shake my head. "I'm sorry, but I can't talk to you about this… I just can't…" I'm growing worried because I can feel a fight approaching, just like the one we had back in December.

"Why not?" he asks, but there's wariness in his voice and I wonder if he already knows what I'm thinking about.

"Because the last time I brought it up we ended up fighting," I say quietly. "And I don't want to fight."

He tenses and I know he's figured out what's been bothering me, that it's about marriage and our future. He lets out a slow breath and I feel like I'm going to cry because I want him to just say it. *Lila, I want you for the long run.* It doesn't have to be *Lila, will you marry me?* I just want to know what's ahead of us, more than just the next few days.

"What can I do to make you feel better?" he asks with sincerity.

I shake my head, sucking back the tears. "Nothing really." And it's the blunt truth because even if I made him say it, if he doesn't mean it, then it's nothing more than words. "Just let me think through my thoughts and figure stuff out…figure out what I want."

I'm not even sure what I mean, but he looks like I've just told him I'm breaking up with him. Frowning, he gets to his feet and picks up his journal. I think he's going to take off, but then he extends his hand to me and helps me to my feet.

"Let's go pack up and hit the road; otherwise we won't have time for the beach," he says, avoiding eye contact with me.

I nod, a lump forming in my throat because I still have no clue where we're headed. To the beach in a few days. Then what? Home. And what happens when we get home? We don't talk about it, so I have no idea. No idea what he wants, if he'll ever want what I want. If maybe we're just wasting our time.

\* \* \*

# Ethan

Lila needs to figure stuff out. Figure out what she wants. What the fuck does that mean? I'm not even sure what the hell just happened between us. One minute I have my fingers inside her because the need to touch her was so overwhelming it was worth getting wet and cold, and then the next thing I know we're arguing and it feels like she might be thinking about breaking up with me. Or wanting to take a break. And I don't want a break. I just want to keep doing what we're doing. I'm having fun and that's all I've ever wanted out of life. To enjoy it.

When I was younger, and pictured my road trip, I'd always pictured doing it myself. But then Lila entered my life and things sort of shifted when I fell in love with her. It was one of the things that made me realize I was in love with her—because being alone didn't seem as appealing as being with her.

After we pack up the truck, we head down the mountain, barely saying more than two words to each other. As I drive down the road, heading toward the town on the outskirts of the mountains, I can't help but wonder if in the future, Lila is going to give me an ultimatum. If she'll demand that I either marry her or she'll leave me... Fuck, what if she just leaves and never even gives me a choice? What if one day I wake up and she's gone? Jesus, I never thought I'd turn into this guy, the one who gets upset at the idea of his girlfriend walking out on him. But after what Lila said on the rock... the idea that she could be thinking about ending it... I've definitely turned into that guy and I'm about to panic. Still, the idea of fully committing is scaring the shit of me too.

"I didn't mean for it to sound like that," Lila suddenly blurts out from the passenger seat, finally turning her head toward me. "Back at the rock... what I said... I'm not trying to figure out what I want. I know what I want—you. And I'm sorry if I made you think I was questioning that."

"Don't be sorry," I say, gripping the steering wheel as I guide my truck around the corner. "You were just being honest, right?"

She shakes her head and inches across the seat toward me. "I wasn't, though... I was just frustrated because I worry... about stuff..."

My eyebrows furrow as I downshift for a steep hill. "About what? Marriage stuff?"

She shrugs and then looks down at her hands as she picks at her fingernails. "I just don't want to end up alone. That's all. I mean, if I don't have you, then all I really have is my sister, but you know how she is—she barely even has time to talk to me on the phone. And Ella's got her own life now."

"You won't ever be alone," I promise, reaching over and taking her hand. "You'll always have me, no matter what happens."

She presses her lips together and it looks like she's on the verge of crying. "I just want to make sure that I have you forever...that you and I"—she glances up at me, gesturing her hand between us—"that this will never change because I don't want it to change. I love being with you, Ethan. Even when I'm filthy and smell like a garbage can."

It's midafternoon and the sunlight reflects in her blue eyes, her blond hair is pulled up in a messy bun on her head, and she's wearing a tank top with no bra and cutoffs. Her eyes are a little wide and have the slightest bit of fear in them because she's basically handing me her emotions to do with as I please.

She's fucking perfect and hearing her say that she doesn't want anything to change between us makes me want to pull the car over and fuck her again and again. Whether I'll admit it aloud or not, I want this—her and I. I want to travel with her. Kiss her. Touch her. Whenever I want. But at the same time I'm terrified. And I hate that I'm so scared of the idea, the idea of wanting someone so much. Yet, I can't help it. I've been through too much—seen too much with my parents—that I get what comes with wanting someone so much. I'd basically be opening myself up to anything, even heartbreak. And Lila too. And the last thing I ever want to do is hurt her. "I want it too," I admit, and she releases a trapped breath in her chest. "But I'm also worried...about what we could become. I just don't want to rush stuff, you know. I don't want to get so caught up in doing what people think they're supposed to do, like..." I trail off, getting a little uncomfortable. "Like getting married and settling down…I don't want to do it too fast and ruin the perfect we have right now."

She nods, understanding, because I've told her enough about my mom and dad and their shitty relationship that she gets my fear of becoming like them. "I know…I'm worried too." She sits back in the seat and faces forward. "My parents weren't that great and the last thing I want to do is become them." She pauses and it makes me nervous, wondering what else she's going to say. "However, at the same time, I look at Ella and Micha and they're so happy."

"I know," I say, and then frown. "But how do we know that we'll be happy instead of angry and sad all the time, like our parents? I just want to make sure that I—that *we*—don't turn out like them. Hating each other…yelling at each other…hurting each other…I want to make sure that we're in the right place where we both want the same things." *And I'm not sure I'm there yet.*

She swallows hard. "Well, we can't know for sure—no one can see the future. We just have to be willing to take the risk."

She waits for me to agree and I want to tell her right then and there that I'm ready to take that risk. That I want to be with her forever, because I know I do, but images of my mom and dad screaming at each other surface and then I picture Lila and me in the same place, yelling at each other because I want one thing and she wants something else. My lips end up staying sealed, refusing to part and just finally say what I want.

I stew in my own regrets for the rest of our journey down the mountain while Lila stares out the window, looking sadder the more time goes by. By the time we reach the small town at the foothills, it's getting late. The sky is bright orange and pink as the sun sets behind us. The few buildings, gas stations, and houses lining the street are shadowed by the mountains and the town is pretty quiet, only a few vehicles driving up and down the street.

"Do you want to stop at that café up there?" I ask, pointing at a small neon sign at the entry to Dina's Café and Diner. Then I force a smile, even though it hurts. "I'm sure you're getting sick of canned food and Pop-Tarts."

She shrugs, finally looking at me for the first time since we stopped talking. I realize she's had her head turned because she's been crying. The evidence of it is all over her bloodshot eyes and red, streaked cheeks and it's all my fault.

"Dinner sounds good, I guess," she says, her voice strained.

I pull the truck into the parking lot and turn off the engine. As she turns to get out of the car, I reach for her arm and stop her. She freezes but doesn't look at me.

"Baby, look at me," I say. Lila is actually the only person I've ever called that, but mainly because she's the only girl I've ever genuinely been in love with, at least in a way that using endearing pet names doesn't seem totally cheesy.

She wipes her eyes with her free hand and then reluctantly turns to me in the seat. It kills me to see the sadness in her eyes. Any other girl and I'd probably have bailed out by now. Too much pressure and heavy emotions, but with Lila, I don't want to lose her. Ever.

I pull her across the seat toward me, not stopping until she's right beside me. Then I take a deep breath and do the best I can to explain how I feel. "I promise I'm not going anywhere. You and I have lots of road trips and fights and hot steamy sex ahead of us." I mentally shake my head at myself. If I was writing it down, it would have sounded a hell of a lot better. "You can even come on the road trip with me to Star Grove if you want. Granted, you'll have to put up with my mom and dad's arguing and shit."

The corners of her lips quirk into an almost smile. "You want me to go with you?"

"I always want you to go with me," I say. "I just hate taking you up there around all the fighting."

"I can handle fighting," she insists, seeming so much happier. "I just want to make sure that you *want* me to come with you."

"Of course I do," I say, tucking a strand of her hair behind her ear. Then I aim a teasing grin at her. "And I'm not going anywhere. As much as you're a pain in the ass, I always want you with me."

Her smile breaks through and she cups my face in her hands and pulls my lips to hers. She kisses me until I become breathless, which is the fucking pussiest thing to say, yet it's fucking happening.

Then she's pulling away, blinking her eyes with a small smile on her lips and all I want to do is hold on to her. "All right, you won me over. I'll drop the whole marriage and future talk for a while."

"You're just going to drop it like that?" I ask, stunned she's making it that easy.

Her shoulders rise and fall as she shrugs. "Yeah, I mean, you said we have a lot of road trips ahead of us and that's all I really wanted to know."

"Yeah, but..." I drift off, wondering why I'm not letting it go, when she's dropping it like I wanted...or thought I'd wanted. But she's got me thinking about stuff and now it seems hard just to stop processing where I see us down the road together. Taking trips. Kissing. Talking. Living in a cabin somewhere in the mountains where I could watch her bathe in a pond all the time. Is that where I see myself? Is that where I see us?

Dammit, where is my head going?

She slides over to the passenger door and hops out of the truck with a spring in her walk and her ass shaking in the pair of cutoffs she's wearing. And I'm left watching her and wondering what the fuck is wrong with my head.

# *Chapter 3*

## Lila

I'm feeling a little bit better, despite the fact that I'm starving. I've never been a fan of cafés but right now I'd settle for anything that didn't come in a box or a can. After we're seated in a booth, I search the menu, my belly grumbling as the waitress fills up our waters. We order our drinks and then I run my fingers along the list of appetizers, singing along with the song playing through the speakers, one that I don't know the name of but have heard a ton of times.

Ethan watches me with a curious expression, the sleeves of his plaid shirt pushed up so I can see all his tattoos and the lean muscles in his arms. "Since when do you know 'Creep' by Radiohead?"

"You're always listening to it," I point out. "And somehow, despite my protest, the lyrics have managed to get themselves stuck inside my head."

He gives me this strange look, like he's realizing something that scares him. Then he fixes his attention on the menu in front of him, his forehead creasing. He reads for a few moments and then lets out a frustrated breath, shutting his menu and turning in the booth toward me. "Okay, was that like some sort of reverse psychology or something?"

I gape at him, confused. "What are you talking about?"

He roughly rakes his fingers through his hair, seeming irritated. "That stuff back in the truck…about being okay with not knowing now…" He lowers his arm onto the table. "About being okay not knowing if we'll be together five or ten years down the road."

"That's not what I meant," I say. "What I meant was that I felt better because you said we had a lot of stuff ahead of us and that's all I really wanted—to know we had some sort of future ahead of us."

He still looks confused, his lips parting, and I can tell he's about to say something that's going to either completely and utterly make me happy for a very long time or break me apart. But then he snaps his jaw shut when the waitress returns to take our orders. I order mozzarella sticks, a chicken sandwich, and piece of chocolate cake, and Ethan orders enough to feed a small village.

"We'll have leftovers for the road," he says after the waitress leaves. "That way we don't have to stop a lot."

I glare at him. "Please. Not the no-stopping-unless-we're-in-dire-need policy. I revoked that after the near-peeing-my-pants accident."

He laughs, recollecting the memory with a thoughtful look on his face. "Hey, there was an upside to that," he says. "I got to watch you pee in a cup."

"You got to see me *try* peeing in a cup," I remind him, narrowing my eyes. "It didn't work."

"Hey, it always works for me," he says, still grinning. "It's not my fault your girl part can't aim right."

I maliciously reach over and grab his manly part, giving it a good rub to mess with his head. "Need I remind you what my girl part can do to your boy part?" I take his hand and put it between my legs; then I smile when he starts to touch me between the legs. We're completely hidden by the table, although the orgasmic look on his face might give us away.

"Never make fun of my girl part again," I say. "And stop calling it a girl part. It's weird."

"What do you want me to call it?" he asks with a dark grin. "Your wet, dripping—"

I slap my hand over his mouth, stifling a laugh. "Not so loud."

Ethan has this thing with never getting embarrassed in public. In fact, one time he proceeded to tell me, in a very loud voice, the various positions he was going to fuck me in over the course of the night. He then proceeded to give me a demonstration of what I was going to sound like when I was coming. We were in a McDonald's and a lot of people weren't very happy about it. Still, he did make good with his word and tried all the positions on me and I did scream out just like he had predicted.

"What are you thinking about?" he asks, his fingers wandering to my side. They dig inward and he guides me closer to him in the booth until I'm practically on his lap.

"How you did me that one night in all those different, crazy positions," I say, biting on my lip when his grip tightens even more and hot tingles course up and down my inner thighs.

Hunger consumes his eyes. "You want to do it again?" he asks. "I've got a ton more positions I can show you."

I bite my lip harder, so hard, in fact, I taste blood in my mouth, feeling the shift in our mood and wanting it more than anything. "But we don't have a hotel room."

He glances around the mostly vacant café like he's almost forgotten where we were. Then his eyes wander to the window at the front of the diner where it's dark, a faint stream of light trickling in from the lampposts in the parking lot. "Why don't we get a room?" he asks, turning his attention back to me.

The look in his eyes pushes me nearly over the edge. I swear if he doesn't tone it down, I'm going to have an orgasm right here at the table, in a restaurant full of people. Granted, it'd be worth it. "I thought we had to hit the road tonight?"

He shakes his head, his expression filling with lust and making my body feel like it's going to combust. "We can still make it back in time…we'll just have to make a few less stops…" His gaze flicks to my breasts. I'm not wearing a bra and my nipples have gotten so hard that they're visible through the thin fabric.

His fingers find them and trace them in soft circular motions, while he waits for me to respond.

"We can do that," I say, but it comes out a groan and his fingers clamp down on me.

The next thing I know we're headed up to the counter, telling the waitress that we'd like our food to go. Then we wait very impatiently, sneaking touches when no one's looking, and sometimes when people are looking, until our food arrives at the counter in to-go bags. Ethan pays and then we leave, driving across the street to this sketchy-looking motel that has about five rooms total. I don't care, though. I just want him now. It's amazing what he can do to me just with the simple promise of being inside me, how far I've come because of him. I remember when sex was just numbing. I felt nothing. Felt like I was too worthless to enjoy it. Then Ethan came along and all that changed. He made me feel alive and worth something.

Almost every moment is perfect with him and hopefully we'll have a thousand more moments just like this.

* * *

# Ethan

Normally, I would have said we didn't have enough time to stay for an extra night, not if I want to stop at all the places I want to on the way home. But all of that stops mattering the moment I start thinking about being inside her. Hell, I'll give up making a stop in Tennessee like I was planning on...see one less mountain as long as I can just touch her a little bit longer.

My dick's so hard it fucking hurts. Touching her like that, especially in public, feels so forbidden and it's such a turn-on, especially when she touches me back. Only Lila can challenge me like that and get me so riled up. I swear to God I was on the verge of peeling her clothes off and slipping inside her right there in the booth. Luckily for the sake of giving everyone in the café a live porn show, we managed to make it across the street to a crappy-looking motel. It's definitely not the best place in the world and I'm a little worried that Lila's going to flip, but as soon as we step into the room, her lips collide with mine and she's stripping off her shirt eagerly.

And just like that I get lost in her; all the stuff bouncing around in my head momentarily dissipates as my tongue explores her mouth. Our bodies line perfectly together as she traces her fingers up my back, shivering when I do the same to her. I sketch the lines of the tattoo on her back as I steer us through the dark toward the bed. Moments later, we stumble backward and the mattress collapses beneath us as we land on it together. I brace my weight onto my arms, her head pinned between them, as I keep kissing her. Her legs drift to my hips and she bends her knees and wraps them around my waist, hitching her ankles behind my back. She starts to grind her hips against me, making my cock go rock-hard. I move with her, letting her veer toward the edge while I try to hang on, wanting to be inside of her so goddamn badly my body is pretty much sweating in desperation, but she's too close to coming and I want to see her lose it before I slip inside her because I enjoy watching her get lost like that, especially when I'm the one doing it to her—making her feel like that. So I keep going, watching, her eyes glazing over. Finally she stops moving with me, her muscles tightening as she cries out. Her head falls back and her eyelids flutter shut as she drifts off, her fingertips delving into my shoulder blades so sharply I feel the skin break.

I've never been so turned on in my life.

"Jesus, Lila," I groan, begging my body to hold on just a little bit longer.

She breathes ravenously, her chest heaving as she blinks lazily. When she looks at me again, she has a content look on her face and a faint smile. "Your turn," she says, and then she nudges me to move.

I more than willingly obey, rolling off her and onto my back. She stands up on the mattress and slips her shorts and panties off, then undoes the button on my shorts and removes them, along with my boxers. She takes a condom out of the back pocket of my shorts before tossing them aside. My hand glides up her leg to her waist, pulling her toward my mouth, but she wiggles out of my grip, tears the condom wrapper open, and puts it on me. Before I can even respond to her touch, she's straddling me and lowering herself onto my cock.

I grip her waist as her warmth surrounds me and I lift my hips and rock inside her, slowly, savoring every single goddamn aspect of the moment.

"God, this feels so good," she mutters in ecstasy as she lets her head fall back and rocks her hips with me.

My hold on her waist tightens as I give another slow thrust into her, deeper this time. "Yeah, it does…"

We start to move rhythmically together, having orgasm after orgasm, getting lost over and over again inside each other. I think we break our record for how many times we have sex in one night—it's five now. Exhausted and sweaty, we finally settle down for the night, holding on to each other as we drift to sleep. She falls asleep first and I end up just watching her breathe softly in my arms, never wanting to move. Never wanting to do anything ever again but this. In fact, I can actually see myself doing this over and over again with her. Every night...

Shit. I'm thinking about the future and I'm so... Confused... This is such a perfect and beautiful moment and I wish I could just stay like this forever with her. Yeah, we're starting the long drive home tomorrow, but I want things to say the same when we get back. I have a revelation as I think about heading home. I meant what I said in the truck. I want more road trips like this with her. I want to hold her in my arms in a shitty motel one day again in the future. I don't want to lose her—I realized that when I thought she was breaking up with me at the rock. I want her and I don't want to be scared to want her so much.

I'm suddenly fucking freaking out as I realize something. My biggest fear is right in front of me and I want to get over it, but I'm not sure I can. Making sure she's still asleep, I get out of bed, go over to my suitcase, and take my journal out. The moment the pen touches the paper, my feelings pour out of me. When I'm done, my hand is shaking, but I have the truth right here in front of me. And I'm not sure if I'm terrified, happy, relieved, or what.

But one thing's for sure. I need to tell Lila.

# *Chapter 4*

## Lila

Last night was amazing to say the least and when morning comes around, I feel like skipping and singing because I feel that happy. But instead we end up going for a hike and I listen to Ethan chat about the wildlife. Sometimes listening to him can be magical, especially when he's just laid back and not overthinking things. It happens a lot when we're hiking.

"I seriously could just live up here and write all day," he admits as he sits down on the top of the hill we just hiked up, stretching his legs out and staring down at the rolling hills and small town below.

I sit down with him and crisscross my legs. There's a gentle breeze blowing through my hair and I have to pluck strands of it out of my mouth. "What would you write about? The view?"

He shakes his head and shrugs, squinting against the sunlight. "I'm not even sure...something, though."

I rest back on my hands and lean my shoulder into his, breathing in his scent of cologne, mixed with campfire and a hint of dirt. "Do you think one day you'd like to become a writer?"

He shrugs again, glancing at me out of the corner of his eye. "I haven't thought that far ahead of what I'm going to do for the rest of my life…what I want to be." He looks down at the ground, seeming confused, and I'm suddenly reminded of the bigger problems ahead of us, ones that I want to shove aside for now.

"Well, maybe one day you should think about what you want to do," I dare suggest. "It could be fun, you know. To write for a living. Well, at least for you since you seem to love it so much."

"You don't even know if I'm good," he says with a smile.

"Well, if you can write like how you talk sometimes, then I'm sure you are." I pause, considering my next words carefully. "Or you could just let me read some of the stuff you wrote." I actually heard him last night when he thought I was asleep, scratching away in his journal, and I wish I knew what he was writing about.

He pauses, biting at his bottom lip, and for a second I think he's considering it. I start to get a little excited and nervous, because I might finally get a full insight into what goes on in that head of his. What he thinks and feels—what he sees when he looks at me.

But then he says, "Trust me. You don't want to read what goes on in my head." And my hopefulness crumbles.

I fake an exaggerated pout. "Yes, I do. I promise. Even if it's bad, I want to know."

He stifles a smile as he leans in and grazes my bottom lip with his fingertip. "Stop pouting to try and get your way," he says, and then he kisses me.

We kiss until we're panting and then we pull away, breathless and sweaty. We relax for a while and look out at the land below us, enjoying the view and the quiet and I know at that moment that he's happy because it's the kind of moment he loves.

"The thing is," Ethan says, startling me. "I don't really write stories. Just my thoughts."

"But isn't that what all stories are?" I ask. "Just someone's thoughts?"

"Yeah, but my journal isn't like a book," he says. "It's just a bunch of rambling about how I feel…about stuff…and my feelings…It's sort of how I discover what I'm really feeling."

"About me?" I sound a little nervous.

He looks even more nervous. "Yeah, sometimes I write about you and how I'm feeling about you." He pauses with his mouth open, like he wants to say more, but then he snaps his jaw shut.

"Do you ever write anything mean about me?" I hold my breath in anticipation.

He shakes his head, looking stunned by my question. "I would never write anything bad about you. Ever."

"Then why can't I read just a page or two?" I ask.

"I'm not sure I can let you," he mumbles. "Not sure if I'm ready yet…" He trails off, staring out at the hills in front of us, looking as lost as we probably do out in the middle of thousands of trees. If it wasn't for him, I'd never be able to find my way back. Thankfully, he has a good sense of direction.

I want to press him more, because I'm really curious what he's writing about all the time, but I can tell his mind's already wandering, so I seal my lips and pretend to be happy. Eventually he starts to get up. I bend my legs to stand up, too, figuring we're leaving, but he puts a hand onto my shoulder and gently pushes me down to the ground. Then he winds around behind me and sits down, putting a leg on each side of me and winding his arms around my waist. He pulls me against him and buries his face into my neck, kissing it. "This past month has been amazing," he whispers, and sucks on my neck, rolling his tongue out, teasing my skin with kisses. "I really wish we could stay this way."

I let my head fall to the side to give him more room to tease my neck. "We can't just live in a tent forever...as much fun as it's been, I really can't wait to have a real roof over my head."

He moves his lips up my neck to my earlobe. "What if we built a cabin for us to live in?"

"Why would we do that?" I ask, breathless as his kisses make my skin dot with goose bumps. "Or better yet, how would we?"

"Save up." He makes a path of kisses down my neck as his hand slips underneath the front of my shirt. "Build one. Move out here. Live. Write. Do whatever the hell we want for the rest of our lives."

My heart hammers inside my chest, wondering if this conversation is headed where I think it's headed. "Forever? Just you and I?" Is he talking about our future?

"Maybe," he says distractedly, and then he presses his fingertips to the side of my jaw and kisses me deeply, leaving me more confused than ever.

But like always, his kisses make me forget my confusion.

* * *

# Ethan

I'm messing this up. Really, really bad. There was a reason why I wanted to take her up here—some things I want to say about us that I discovered last night—but now I'm chickening out and panicking. I suddenly feel like I'm fourteen again and the weight of the world—the pressure—is building up and crushing me. I need to calm down.

I start kissing her as a way around it, knowing that eventually I'll have to break the kiss and finally just tell her how I feel.

About us. About our future. But I kiss her for as long as possible, until she's gasping against my mouth and I'm gently pulling at her hair. I can tell we're only a few more heated moments away from peeling off our clothes and having sex right here on the trail. It wouldn't be the first time, and yet I carefully pull away, nibbling on her lip before sitting up straight.

She looks flustered. "What's wrong?" Her fingers travel up the front of my chest to the top of my shirt, where she grips at the fabric, trying to guide me back to her. "Don't you want to relive the Fourth of July incident?"

I smile as I recollect the Fourth of July. Fireworks exploding over the lake in front of us. Trees surrounding us. Hiding under a blanket, listening to people chatter in the distance as we made love, knowing that at any moment someone could walk up the trail and see us. Neither of us really cared. In fact, it made things more exhilarating.

"Not just yet," I say, cupping her cheek. "I actually need to talk to you about something."

Her forehead creases as she sits up, then kneels and turns to face me. "It's not bad, is it?"

"As long as I can get it out right, it isn't." I let out a loud exhale, preparing to do something I never thought I'd do. "The thing is, you keep talking about marriage and stuff and it really freaks me out," I tell her, and when she frowns I quickly add, "But it's not like I don't think about where we're going to be down the road… if we're going to end up together… be together forever." I put my hands on her thighs as she watches me with worry. "I actually think about it a lot. More than I actually realized… Something that I sort of discovered after writing last night."

"And what did writing reveal to you?" she asks, biting on her bottom lip as I smooth my thumb across her cheek.

"That you and I will end up together." I swallow hard, hating that I have to add the last part, but I need to if I'm going to be honest. "However, I don't think we should get married soon."

She rolls her eyes, which wasn't the response I was expecting. "I don't think we should get married soon either," she says, inching closer to me. "I just wanted—no *needed*—to know we're headed somewhere that could maybe lead to that one day. And that you feel the same way as I do about being together in the long run."

I tangle my fingers through her hair "You know I love you, right?"

"Yes," she says, leaning in for a kiss. "And I love you too."

I pull her in for a quick kiss and then rest my forehead against hers, shutting my eyes, preparing myself for the next thing I'm going to say. Something that terrifies the shit out of me because it's so permanent and the even scarier part is that I want it to be. "I want to do something."

She catches her breath. "What?"

I slip my hand up the back of her shirt and place my palm over her tattoo on her back. "I think...I mean, I want to get another tattoo."

I feel her lashes flutter against me as she opens her eyes and slants away. I open my eyes but keep my hand on her back right between her shoulder blades. She's giving me a baffled look, her eyes wide and searching mine.

"I don't get it," she says. "How do we go from our future talk to you getting a tattoo? I mean, if you want to get another tattoo, that's totally okay with me. You look hot with them...but I don't—"

Chuckling under my breath, I cover her mouth with my hand. "Lila, I meant that *we* should get tattoos together. Ones to mark this trip. And the beginning of our future...ones that sort of go together." When she looks like she's starting to relax, I remove my hand from her mouth. "I knew this couple with really cool matching bands on their fingers and I thought maybe we could get something like that."

"You want to get a matching tattoo with me," she says, a little shocked. "But it's so permanent."

"That's sort of the point." I pause, wondering why she's not excited about this. I thought she would be, but maybe I've been reading her wrong. "We don't have to. I just thought..." I trail off as she gets to her feet and starts to walk toward the trail.

I quickly get to my feet and hurry after her. "Where are you going?"

She glances over her shoulder at me, heading toward the trees at the bottom of the hill. "I want you to show me what you wrote last night."

My expression falls. "Why?"

She turns around, walking backward with a grin on her face. "I want to see how you really feel—I want to make sure that you're not just doing this for me because I've been pressuring you. That you really want this as much as I do. And if it does seem that you want to make that sort of leap with me, then I'll totally do it, but if not, then..." She turns around as she reaches a steep spot on the hill where the ground gets a little loose.

"And if you don't think I want this, then what?" I ask, catching up with her and placing my hand on her back to help her down the steep slope.

"Then we won't get the tattoos right now," she says, stumbling a little, and my fingers enfold her waist to catch her from falling.

"But I thought you wanted a commitment?" I ask, taking her hand as we reach the flat section at the bottom of the hill.

"I do," she says as we duck to enter the trees. "But I also want to know for sure that *you* want it. And if you do, then great, and if you're not ready for it, then you're not ready for it."

I grow a little nervous. "But what if what I wrote freaks you out?"

She aims a disbelieving look at me. "Are you kidding me? After all the stuff I put you through, you think that something you wrote in your journal is going to freak me out?" She pauses as we reach the open section of the trail where the trees are sparse. "You helped me through addiction, family problems, and helped me find myself. I don't think anything you wrote could be more intense than that."

"I wouldn't go that far," I say, unsure if I want her to read anything in my journal. It's like giving her insight straight into my head.

"If you don't want me to, then that's fine," she says. "But I'm not going to get matching tattoos until I know for sure that you want this and aren't just saying so because I've been weird about commitment lately."

"I never say anything but the truth," I remind her. "Even if it's harsh." I pause, tugging my free hand through my hair, thinking about what I want and what I don't want and which one is more important. But in the end only one thing matters—what she wants. "I'll let you read it…but just prepare yourself…I always write what I say and sometimes…well, I'm not sure how you're going to interpret it…whether you're going to see it as me wanting a future with you."

She swallows hard and then lets out a loud exhale, looking nervous. "Well, I guess we're about to find out."

# Chapter 5

## Lila

I don't want to get too happy just yet. I need to make sure that he wants something linked to me branded on his gorgeous body forever. I don't think that Ethan would ever lie to me, especially with something this big. He's always been really truthful in the past, but the only way I'll be able to truly know is if I read his words.

He looks nervous as we sit in his truck, the sun glaring in through the windows. He's flipping through the pages of his journal, searching for the right page, and I try to stay calm in the passenger's seat, hoping there's nothing in there that's going to upset me.

He finally stops flipping through the pages and takes a deep breath before he looks up at me. "Just make sure you read the whole thing. It starts off kind of"—he struggles for the right words—"unsure in the beginning, but it gets better."

I nod and then reach across the seat toward the journal. He glances at it one more time, seeming torn, before he reluctantly hands it over. I take it and put it on my lap, feeling a little uneasy as I read the first word on the page: *confusion*.

"Just start right here?" I ask, tapping the top of the page with my finger.

He nods and then turns toward the window, staring at the vacant motel parking lot to the side of us. I swallow hard, tell myself to go into this with an open mind, and then with caution, I start to read.

Confusion. That's what I feel every time I think about the future. I hate thinking about where I'm going to be in a few years—where I'm supposed to be. If I had my way, I'd take things day by day. Never think about the next day or about the past. I'd live life in the moment. Breathe it. Live freely. It's so much less stressful than worrying all the time about where I'm going to be down the road or who I'm going to be with. I already lost someone once that I cared for. And the idea of losing Lila is like a hundred times worse than that. I'm not even sure if I could get over her if I tried. And what if I didn't lose her, but we just ended up despising each other like my parents and her parents do. That would be equally as hard. It seems so much easier just to stay away from that deep of a commitment and avoid all the "what ifs."

The problem is it's sort of selfish to think this way about life, especially when I'm not the only one in my life. Lila is such a huge part of me. She's more than that. Over these last couple of years, she's become my best friend and not opening up to her completely because of my fears is wrong. She's the person I love more than anyone else in this world and if I have to open my eyes for a moment, and look forward, all I see is her. God, it's the truth…She's all I want. That much I know. I never want anyone else to go through all this shit with me—to go through life with me. And if I have to decide one thing right now about my future, it's that I want to be with her. I want her with me. Even five or ten years down the road. Even when we're thirty or forty. Even if it means we could possibly turn out like our parents, I want to try. I want to try to have a future with her. What the hell happens between now and then I'm not so sure. But do I even need to be sure about that yet? Maybe I only need to be sure about one thing. And that's her and I always being together. Even through the shitty times. I'd never go back and change a damn thing. Every single thing that we've been through has gotten us to this moment where she's lying in the bed beside me and just her being here makes me so content. I breathe easier. I don't even want to think about being on this trip alone. Yeah, I love the quiet, but it could never compare to all the moments we've shared together. Fireworks. Arguments. Ponds. Kisses. Sex…God the sex is great. Every conversation with her, good and bad. Every moment, light and dark. I want to relive it over and over again. I want so many more moments and conversations.

I want this to be permanent. I want Lila and I to be permanent.

Forever and Always.


I try not to cry. I really do. But I'm an emotional person and this…well, I never ever thought anyone would ever feel this way about me.

As my tears start to stain his beautiful words, I quickly shut the journal so the ink stays intact. I quickly wipe my tears with my hand, look up at him, and before he can speak, I say, "So where are we going to get the tattoos?"

\* \* \*

# Ethan

I wasn't sure how she'd take what I wrote. Yeah, the ending was good, but the beginning…well it was full of my fears. And then she starts to cry and I'm a little worried she's maybe misunderstood what I was trying to convey in my journal. I'm about to ask her what's wrong, but then she says she wants to go get the tattoos. I'll admit I'm a little scared, but in a terrifyingly good way. I want this. I knew it the moment I wrote the word *permanent*.

After we decide to get the tattoos, I drive us over to a tattoo shop on the main section of town between a row of shops. We go inside and start looking through the examples on the wall, but Lila keeps frowning at them.

"I want something that we come up with," she says, resting her arms on top of the glass countertop. "Something that's just yours and mine."

"A symbol?" I ask. "Or words?"

"Words," she says, smiling. "I think you should come up with words that connect us."

I point at myself. "Why does it have to be me?"

"Because." She walks up to me and hooks her arms around my neck. "You put words together beautifully. I seriously think you should consider the whole writer thing."

I press back a smile, feeling my heart speed up with panic and fear and excitement. "One future move at a time, please," I say, and she laughs. I let a slow breath ease past my lips as I try to think of something to put on our fingers. There's not a lot of room and I know the artist is probably going to tell us that more than one word is too much. I think about the last words I wrote in my journal and how they were so huge because they made me realize that moving forward with Lila was something I wanted.

"How about forever and always?" I say, taking her hand in mine and tracing my finger around her ring finger.

She glances down at her hand, puzzled. "What, you take *forever* and I take *always*? But then who would take the word *and*?"

I shrug. "How about both of us."

She glances up at me with her brows knit. "You want to split up *and*? Like you take the *a* and half the *n* and then I take the other half and the *d*?" she asks, and I nod. "Wouldn't that look a little weird?"

"Does it really matter if it looks weird?" I ask. "It'd mean something to us and that's all that matters, right?"

She considers what I said and then a smile breaks through. "I really love that idea." She pulls me in toward her and we kiss until a very bulky dude with tattoos covering his arms comes into the waiting room to see what we want. When I explain it to him, he looks at me like I'm some sort of punk kid who's stupidly in love. I don't really give a shit what he thinks, though, and feel perfectly content with his disgusted look as he draws up the designs.

When he's finished, I decide to go first since Lila seems nervous, like she was when she got her first and only tattoo. I take a seat and the guy puts the drawing on me, making sure it's where I want it. When we get it in the correct place, he gets the needle ready and I shut my eyes, feeling myself change the moment the ink touches my skin. I can feel myself moving forward with each stroke. Feel myself connecting to Lila. Feel that I'm exactly where I want to be. Right in this moment with her.

* * *

# Lila

I get so nervous around needles. It took a lot just to get me in the chair for the first and only tattoo I've ever gotten. Then I damn near fainted the first minute into it. But Ethan stood by my side and reminded me why I decided to do it. Because I want to be free and wanted to have something that would forever represent my journey toward freedom.

But watching Ethan mark his finger with something that would always connect him to me is different. It makes me feel even more free and alive. Excited. Overwhelmed. Loved. It's the perfect moment that ends too quickly because suddenly he's finished and it's my turn.

"You sure you want to do this?" he teases, stretching out his fingers as we trade places.

I eagerly and very anxiously nod as I plop down in the leather chair. The large guy with a lot of colorful tattoos on his arms who did Ethan's tattoo tells me to put my hand up on the armrest. He seems sort of cranky, but I don't care. Nothing could ever ruin this moment, not even a cranky guy who smells like he's in dire need of some deodorant.

I stay quiet as he positions the drawing on my finger until he gets it in the right place. Ethan holds my hand the entire time, while staring down at his free hand. The skin around the tattoo is a little red, but other than that it looks perfect.

*He's perfect.*

He's the only person who's every fully understood me. The only person I've ever trusted. The only person who saw who I really am and the potential of what I could become. He loved me in a way that I thought wasn't possible and that's what I keep telling myself over and over again as the tattoo artist presses the tip of the needle to my finger.

I've gone through a lot over the last eight months or so. I've changed for the better. I've had a lot of moving, life-changing moments. But this one is different. This one is epic. I can feel it through the blissful pain that makes me hyperaware of what I'm doing. And when I'm finished, I feel genuinely happy even though my finger aches.

"So?" Ethan says as I get up from the chair. He watches me, like he's waiting for me to say I regret it.

I stare down at my ring finger with a big grin on my face. I've always pictured myself with a huge diamond on my ring finger, a carat at least, but now…well, this feels so much better. So much more personal and intimate. Nothing could mark our relationship better than this.

I glance up at him, looking him straight in the eye. "I think it's perfect."

He smiles back at me and then slips his fingers through mine. It makes the area of the tattoo sting a little, but there's no way I'm going to pull back. We pay for the tattoos and walk hand in hand outside to his truck.

"You ready to start our journey back home?" he asks, opening the truck door for me.

I nod as I climb in. "I'm ready for anything."

There's a sparkle in his eyes as he leans in, pausing when our lips are only inches apart. "Me too."

He kisses me passionately before pulling away, blinking his

eyes with a dazed look on his face. "We'll have to go on one of these trips every year," he says as he starts to shut the door. "Just you and me and the road. Living in a tent and eating camp food again. Taking baths in the pond." He grins. "Having sex on the shore of a lake, hiding under a blanket."

I smile, feeling happier than I've ever been because I know Ethan will be in my future and that's all I ever wanted, and as long as I have him, nothing else matters. "Sounds perfect."

*Delilah: The
Making of Red*

# Prologue

If you think this is some kind of love story, you're wrong. It's not at all. Does it contain hearts, kisses, and passionate moments between a boy and a girl? Yeah, maybe, but maybe not. It all depends on how you interpret lovey-dovey stuff. If you'd asked me five years ago, when I was a naïve sixteen-year-old, I would have told you this story was leading to all of that. That by the end of my journey I'd be happy and riding off into the sunset with Prince Charming at my side, the love of my life, who always whispered sweet nothings in my ear and told me how wonderful I was.

Because that's how things are supposed to go when you meet that one guy who looks at you like you mean everything to him. Who looks at you like you mean something. Who makes you feel like you're the sunshine in his darkness. Who notices you and makes you feel like the center of the world.

Five years ago, I truly believed that's where my life was going. There were so many possibilities blossoming in the beginning stages of becoming a woman. But I was clueless about love, happiness, life. I was clueless about who I was.

And now I'm lying half-dead on the riverbank, barely able to breathe, unable to move, knowing that if someone doesn't find me soon, I'm going to die here with my soul sucked away, a skeleton of myself. Left for dead at twenty-one years old, a shell of who I used to be five years ago, when I was sixteen, when this all started.

Looking back, I can see the exact moment my life headed in this direction. The one where I was no longer Delilah, but Red.

It was a hot, record-breaking summer, full of possibilities—full of promise. The moment I put the red dress on, I could feel something was about to happen, felt myself transforming into someone else. The dress matched my fiery red hair, high heels, and a string of pearls. I had a gorgeous tan and my breasts had finally grown big enough that I had cleavage. I felt on fire when I looked at my reflection. Beautiful. Different. There was so much hope. Possibilities. I could actually spread my wings and fly.

But eventually I would crash and burn. Because after I got what I wanted, I lost it all and started my slow descent. And at the end of my journey, I'd go down in flames and pay the ultimate price for my choices.

# Chapter 1

# Poison Ivy

*Delilah, sixteen years old…*

*Delilah.* Seductress. Temptress. A treacherous woman. These are just some of the meanings linked to my name. But am I any of them? No, not even close. In fact, I might be the exact opposite.

My mother, on the other hand, is a prime example of these meanings.

She's a complicated woman, who has a lot of ups and downs. She likes to look sexy and young just as much as she likes to yell when she's stressed. Whether it's over bills, her job, or the simple fact that she can't find the right pair of socks, it seems like hollering is her way of letting all the anger out. But the one thing she never refuses to yell about is men. It's her cardinal rule: *Never let men own you—own them.*

It's not like she's a terrible mother. She puts a roof over my head. Feeds me. Gives me clothes and spare money when she has it. She pays for me to take ballet lessons, even though I know she can't afford it. We used to do things together too, but then my father divorced her after twenty-one years of marriage because he didn't love her anymore. Those were his exact words.

She was forty-one. After three months of being divorced, my father remarried a twenty-six-year-old. Then began my mother's desperate search for her fountain of youth. Metaphorically speaking.

She discovered it in bars, cheap dates, and one-night stands with men half her age. I honestly have no idea how she does it—how she manages to wrangle some of the guys home that she does—other than maybe she's living a double life as Poison Ivy, a seductress with a potent kiss that stuns men into a delusional state so she can lure them into her bed.

My mother's not bad looking at all. In fact, she's sort of mesmerizing to look at, although I've never been able to pinpoint exactly what it is about her that's so striking. Her hair is still its original honey blond, her skin has minimal wrinkles, and her boobs don't sag. But she doesn't look twenty-five either, which is around the age of a lot of guys that she brings home. Like the one she brought home last night. He's young, maybe not even twenty-five, with shaggy brown hair, baby blue eyes, and a decent-looking face. He's wearing a button-down shirt, slacks, and a red tie, but the fabric is wrinkly and the clothes are too big, like he's playing dress up in his dad's clothes.

I study him as he eats breakfast at our kitchen table—my mother always cooks them breakfast the morning after—trying to read his thoughts as he eats his bacon and eggs, trying to figure out why he ended up here. Trying to figure out how she does it: makes guys give her that stupid doe-eyed look, because the only looks I've ever gotten from guys are the you're invisible look, the not-interested look, and the you're-such-a-good-friend look. To almost everyone, I'm Invisible Woman.

"Delilah, get yourself something to eat," my mother says, rinsing out the pan in the sink. She's wearing a silk robe that barely reaches her thighs, and it's untied, revealing that she's wearing a lacy nightie underneath that her boobs nearly pop out of. It's not a big deal to me though. In fact, usually she only has a bra and pair of panties on, so I'm grateful for the nighty. Plus she looks good in it. If I looked like that, then I'd probably walk around in a nighty all the time too.

"Oh, yeah, okay," I say, tearing my thoughts away from her outfit and reaching for the bacon on the table.

She raises her brow, giving me a suspicious look, like she's thinking I'm going to seduce the guy she spent the last night with, live up to my name. But I wouldn't even know how to if I wanted to.

"What?" I ask her innocently, stuffing my mouth with bacon.

She rolls her eyes at me and returns to scrubbing down the pan, while the guy across from me wolfs down his bacon. "It's nothing," my mom replies, turning off the faucet. Then she turns around and glances at the clock on the wall. "Aren't you supposed to be headed to school?"

I look over at the time on the microwave. "I have like fifteen minutes."

"Yeah, but I have some things to do," she tells me, staring at her latest conquest like he's the bacon and she wants to eat him up.

The guy looks up at her, ruffling his hair with his hand, and he's looking in my direction, but at the same time he's not really looking at me, more like looking through me. I lean to the side, just to see if I can catch his eye and his attention. I fail epically, and in the end he ends up looking over at my mother. And once again I feel insignificant.

It's like watching a play and my mom is center stage, the spotlights are all on her. Her eyes meet the guy's from across the room. Lust fills their expressions. I can almost visualize my mom growing vines of poison ivy on her body that slide across the floor and tie around his legs and arms, binding him to her.

He stares at her like she's the most amazing, beautiful woman in the world, the way I wish a guy would look at me, just once. "You ready to give me round two, babe?" he asks, forcing an overly large mouthful of bacon down his throat.

I scrunch my nose. This is not going to go well. My mother doesn't like losing control. Doesn't like giving anything to men, only taking.

My mom ties the belt around the robe and closes it up. "Actually, I was thinking about taking you home. I've got to go into work early, and unless you want to take the bus back to the bar to pick up your car, you're going to have to leave with me."

You'd think from what she just said she'd be done with him, but she's not. It's a routine for her. A seductress routine, full of toxic kisses and mind manipulation. She stands up straight and she's wearing heels, so her legs look really long as she struts over to the table and traces her finger across the back of the guy's neck. I catch him shudder. She leans down and whispers something in his ear, then she pulls away, but not before she snatches hold of his tie. His eyes widen as she guides him up, and then he lets her lead him into the bedroom like a dog.

Seconds later I hear the door shut and then music turns on. She always turns music on, either because she likes to listen to it while she has sex or she doesn't want me to hear what's going on. "Leather and Lace" by Stevie Nicks and Don Henley flows down the hallway.

The song continues to play as I finish off my breakfast, then put my dishes away and dance my way back to my room, singing the lyrics under my breath, pretending for a moment that I'm center stage.

I change out of my pajamas and get ready for school. Jeans and a T-shirt are my normal attire. A ponytail is my go-to hairdo. Add a little gloss and eyeliner and I'm good to go. It's not like I'd benefit from trying any harder. Guys don't notice me even when I try. Like the one and only time I wore a bikini to the town pool. I was thirteen and still filling out a little bit, but still I thought it'd be nice if a few guys looked in my direction. But Sandy Manderlin, the lifeguard, was wearing her bikini that day, and let's just say that she could give Pamela Anderson a run for her money.

I felt stupid for even trying and severely inadequate, especially when Tommy Linford told me that I didn't need to wear a bikini at all—that Band-Aids would have sufficed. I retorted with a simple remark about him needing to stuff socks in his swim shorts just to make it seem like he had something there.

He flipped me off and I went home crying. And burned the bikini.

After I get dressed, I slip my Converse sneakers on then throw my pointe shoes and leotard into my backpack because I have dance class after school. The instructor's not the best, not like the instructor over in Fairview who's actually been part of a company and danced on stage in New York City. But she's cheap and it's all my mom can afford. And even getting her to pay for classes, took a lot of persuading and promises to clean the house.

After I get my dance and school stuff, I head outside. It's a bright day, the sun beaming in the sky, birds chirping. It's a scene straight out of *Sleeping Beauty*, except for the forest is a bunch of low-income houses and the animals are crackheads, prostitutes, and poor unfortunate souls who've either had crap luck throughout their life, made bad choices, or, like me and my mom, gotten divorced and lost half of their household income because some deadbeat father won't pay child support.

Still, I pretend I'm Sleeping Beauty because it makes the walk

to school easier, and by the time I've reached the end of the driveway I'm twirling along with my arms out in front in my "in first"
position as I sing "Beautiful Day" by U2.

Halfway to the street, I swear I feel someone watching me, but
shrug it off because no one ever notices me.

I'm in midturn when I hear someone say, "Well, aren't you just
a bunch of rainbows and sunshine." The sound of the male voice
causes me to trip over my next turn. I stumble and fall forward,
slamming my elbow against the chain-link fence bordering the
side of the driveway.

"Motherfucker," I curse in a very unladylike tone as I rub my
scraped elbow

"I'm sorry," the male voice says. "I didn't mean to scare you."

My eyes lift to the house next door, and I find the most gorgeous guy I've ever seen standing near the fence with grease on
his hands and forehead, looking at me. He's got dark brown hair
that's shaved short, and he's wearing a pair of loose-fitting jeans
hanging on his hips and brown work boots. He's also shirtless
and his chest is cut with lean muscles and there's a series of tattoos
on his side that look like tribal art.

Tattoos that I'm staring at.

And he notices me staring too.

I blush, staring down at the sidewalk as I take a few steps back,
squirming under his penetrating gaze. "You didn't scare me," I lie.
"I'm just a klutz."

"You're not a klutz at all," he says, and the sound of his deep
voice sends vibrations through my body. "I was actually enjoying
watching you dance."

I glance up at him, shocked to find he's still looking at me with
so much intensity it's hard to breathe. I search my mind for something to say, but my throat feels very dry.

"In fact, you're probably the complete opposite of a klutz," he continues, looking at me in a way that I've always dreamed a guy would look at me—like I'm not invisible or insignificant. Like I exist.

"What's your name?" he asks, slanting forward toward the fence and resting his elbows on top of it.

"Delilah Peirce," I tell him, shifting my backpack high on my shoulder. "What's yours?"

"Dylan Sanderson." He nods at my single-story stucco house that still has Christmas lights on it even though it's May. "You live there?"

I nod. "Yeah, with my mom."

"Aw." He arches his brows. "So that blond woman I saw earlier coming out to get the paper off the steps is your...sister."

I frown, feeling my invisibility surfacing again, the lights around me dimming, no longer center stage. "No, she's my mom."

His eyebrows shoot up even higher. "Wow, I wasn't expecting that one...how old is she?"

I'm battling to keep my disappointment contained. "Forty-one."

He pauses, studying me intently, and it makes my skin heat, but not from blushing. It heats with want, because I want him to keep looking at me like that. "How old are you?"

"Seventeen." I'm not sure why I lie, other than being seventeen suddenly seems a hell of a lot better than being sixteen, and besides, I think he's a little bit older. "How old are you?"

"Almost eighteen," he says, eyes still on me.

"Did you just move in?" I ask. "Or are you staying with the couple that lives here? I don't remember them moving out."

"They didn't." He hitches his finger over at the house. "I just moved back in with my parents for a little bit until I can figure some stuff out."

I dare to step closer to the fence and notice how beautiful his eyes are. And how much emotion they carry. Like he's feeling too much, but trying to keep it all bottled up inside and hidden from the world. "Well, where'd you live before?"

He seems to get a little tense from this question, his shoulders stiffening. "Here and there."

I think about asking him what his story is, or, better yet, dazzling him with my flirting skills. But I haven't discovered them yet, so instead I end up saying, "That sounds cool."

He gives me a look like he thinks I'm adorable. "Where are you heading to so early in the morning?"

"School," I tell him.

"It's summer. Isn't school out?"

I shake my head. "Today's the last day."

"And you're going?" he questions, wiping the grease on his hands onto his jeans, seeming to lose interest in me as he gazes off over my shoulder. "Man, I used to always ditch the last day."

I suddenly feel like a ten year old with LOSER stamped on my forehead. "Well, I have dance right after and I take the bus from school so I sort of have to go." I make a lame excuse.

"You're a dancer?" he asks, and it brightens me up a little bit that he's paying attention to me again.

I nod. "Yeah, I do mostly ballet and sometimes hip-hop."

His gaze slowly scrolls over my lean legs and flat stomach, and I struggle not to look away from the heat in his eyes and the heat surfacing in my body. The heat only amplifies when his gaze meets mine, and for a moment I feel this strange confidence inside me flicker and I stand up a little bit taller.

"I'd love to see you dance sometime," he says with a smile. I'm not sure how to respond, nervous over the idea. The smile starts to leave his face the longer I stay quiet. "Unless you don't want to."

"No, I want to," I say quickly. "I-I will."

His grin returns, bigger, bolder, more confident. "I'm going to hold you to that, Delilah," he says. "In fact, I'm looking forward to it." He pauses, his eyes skimming over my body again, and then he opens his mouth to say something. The look in his eyes makes me wonder if it's important, but he snaps his jaw shut when a woman walks out the door.

She's wearing a robe, but it's not like my mom's; this woman's robe is made of pink furry material and flows all the way to her ankles. Her hair is in rollers and she has slippers on. "Dylan, get your ass in here and clean up the goddamn mess you left in the kitchen!" she shouts, loud enough that the neighbor across the street can hear.

Dylan's jaw tightens, the bottled emotion in his eyes on the verge of bursting out. "I'll be in there in a minute," he replies in a surprisingly calm tone. He doesn't look at her when he speaks; his gaze is still fixed on me, and all the emotion inside him is directed at me.

It's overwhelming, and my breath hitches in my throat.

"Don't give me that 'I'll be in there in a minute' bullshit," she shouts back, scooping up the newspaper from the porch. "With you that means your dumb ass is going to sit out here and work on the car until you feel like coming in." She backs for the door. "I'm not putting up with your bullshit. Get your ass in here now and quit bothering the goddamn neighbors." She turns away and steps back into the house, the screen door slamming behind her.

There's this long pause where all I can hear is the sound of Dylan breathing. I want to ask him if he's okay, because his mom seems like a real bitch.

Finally, I manage to gather up enough courage. "Are you okay?"

He blinks, like he's stunned, but the stricken look on his face swiftly vanishes and suddenly he looks calm. "I'm perfectly fine. It's nothing I haven't heard before."

"Are you sure?" I double-check. "I know how much of a pain parents can be."

He nods, looking at me as if he's trying to figure something out. "I'll be okay, as long as you can do one thing for me."

"Okay," I say, a little confused.

"When you get home, make sure to say hi to me."

"What if you're not outside?"

"I will be," he promises with a smile, and the dark cloud that rose over him evaporates.

"Okay," I tell him, holding back a smile, despite how much happiness is bubbling up inside me. "I'll make sure I do that."

"Good." His smile broadens. "I'll let you get to school. Wouldn't want you to be late for your last day." He winks at me as he backs away toward an old car parked in the driveway with the hood up.

I wave at him and then head off to school, taking even strides, despite how much I want to dance up the sidewalk. I can feel him watching me all the way to the end of the yard where he can no longer see me as I disappear around the corner.

I let my smile break through. For once someone was looking at me. For once I feel like Poison Ivy instead of Invisible Woman.

Looking back at it now as I lie here on the shore, the water rising with the current and slowly rushing over my body, I realize that I was naïve. That I was nowhere close to being Poison Ivy. That I would never even come close. If anything, Dylan was Poison Ivy in disguise, and I was his next victim.

But it wasn't all his fault. After all, I'm the one who chose to go back to him, even after I discovered his toxic kiss.

# Chapter 2

# Plastic Dolls

I make sure to say hi to Dylan on my way home. We talk for about ten minutes and then he has to go inside to help his mother with something. I don't run into Dylan again for the next couple of days after that, and I'm surprised how sad this makes me. I've never been a girl who obsesses about boys, yet I find myself constantly checking to see, if by chance, he's wandered out to his driveway again.

But three days after we meet, I still haven't seen him again, and it looks like the start to a very long, boring summer. Bryant, my only real close friend, moved clear across the country a few days before school got out. That leaves me to hang out with Martha for the entire summer, who's more Bryant's friend than mine, and who I'm pretty sure thinks my mother is a prostitute.

"I can't believe she walks around like that," Martha says, flipping through a magazine while lying on her stomach on my bed. She's got her brown hair pulled up in a messy bun, shorts and an overly large T-shirt on, and her sunglasses on her head. She could probably be pretty if she tried, but she doesn't. Plus, I think she's an extreme feminist and hates dresses and skimpy clothes. Maybe that's why she's so repulsed by my mom's wardrobe.

"Yeah, you get used to it, though," I tell her, leaning forward in the chair in front of my vanity to peek out the curtain again. I have the perfect view into Dylan's driveway, but like the ten other times I looked out, it's vacant. I sigh, sitting back down, knowing I should stop looking because I'm veering toward stalker behavior.

"I don't think you should have to get used to it," she says. "She's a mom and she should act like one."

I get a little defensive. "Just because she dresses skimpy doesn't mean she's a bad mom."

She glances up at me with doubt. "She's setting a bad example for you and teaches you everything a woman shouldn't be."

"And how do you know what a woman should be?" I ask, knowing I'm being rude, but at the same time she's insulting my mother and she didn't abandon me like my father did. "You're completely clueless about what guys want, which is why you've never gone out on a date."

She glares at me as she closes the magazine. "You know what? I don't have to put up with this," she says, climbing off the bed and slipping on her flip-flops. "I told Byrant I'd try to be nice to you and give you the benefit of the doubt that you'd return the favor, but as usual, you're being a bitch."

"I'm the one being a bitch?" I say, irritated. "You were insulting my mom."

She snatches her purse off the bedpost and gives me a harsh look as she swings it over her shoulder. "I wasn't insulting her. I was just saying what everyone else in the town says about her—that she's a whore." She looks at me condescendingly. "Only I was trying to use nicer words." She heads toward the door and I let her leave, even though I know that there's a good chance I'm going to be spending the entire summer alone now.

"Bitch," I mutter under my breath as I get up and cross my room to the phone on my nightstand. My mom gave me the phone when I was eight, back when I was still into dolls, and so the receiver is pink and glittery and looks like it belongs in Barbie's Dreamhouse. I've been trying to get her to get me a cell phone, but she says we can't afford it.

I dial Bryant's number and wait for him to answer.

"Hey, how's the sexiest redhead in the world?" he asks, which is how he always answers. We're still pretty close, but we actually used to be closer until he started dating someone a few months ago and the girl thought I was some sort of threat, especially when she asked Bryant if we'd ever hooked up and he stupidly told her the truth: that yes, one time when we were fifteen, and tried drinking for the first time, we made out and touched each other inappropriately. After that she didn't want him hanging out with me. He still did hang out once in a while, but not nearly as much as he used to.

"Did you tell Martha to try and give me the benefit of the doubt?" I ask, plopping down onto my bed and staring up at the ceiling at a poster of *Flashdance*, which is totally eighties, but as a dancer I can respect the movie.

"Shit, she told you that?" He curses under his breath and I smile to myself, knowing that if nothing else, Bryant's going to chew her out for doing so.

"Yeah, after she told me that she wasn't going to do it anymore," I tell him, twisting the phone cord around my finger. "And that I was a bitch."

"And were you being a bitch?" he asks.

"Maybe," I admit. "But she called my mom a whore."

He pauses. "But she kind of is."

"Yeah, I know, but it doesn't give her the right to say it."

He sighs. "I know. I'll talk to her."

"Don't bother." I roll onto my side and prop my elbow onto the mattress so I can rest my head against my hand. "I know you want us to get along, but without you, it just feels awkward."

"But I worry about you," he tells me. "You don't have a lot of friends, and I'm worried that you'll just sink."

"You make me sound suicidal," I reply. "And I'm not."

"I know you're not," he replies. "But you can be self-destructive when you're by yourself."

"How do you figure?" I ask, not sure whether I'm curious or offended.

"Remember when I went on that family vacation during the summer," he says. "When we were thirteen."

I frown at the memory. "I was going through a phase."

"Delilah, you almost got arrested."

"I was bored," I argue. "And Milly Amerson was the only one who would spend time with me. It wasn't my fault she was a klepto."

"But it was your fault you tried to be a klepto. And a very bad one at that," he says. "You chose to do it because you were bored and have such a hard time making friends. In fact, you're better at making enemies than anything."

I sigh heavyheartedly. "All right, I get your point," I say. "Sheesh, you're such a mom."

"Well, someone has to be," he says. With anyone else I'd get offended, but I always let Bryant off the hook because he was there right after the divorce when my mom hit rock bottom and she drank herself into depression and would barely get out of bed for three months. She did eventually get up, though, and start taking care of me again, and people are allowed to break every once in a while.

"Thanks for taking care of me," I say. "But I promise, even if Martha and I don't hang out, I'm not going to go back to my klepto days with Milly."

"Just be careful," he says. "I worry about you."

"I know you do," I tell him. "But I promise, if things get too bad, I'll let you know."

"Good," he says. "Now, I gotta go. My mom's nagging at me to help her finish unpacking."

"Okay, call me when you get a chance," I say. "And I'll tell you about my hot neighbor."

He laughs. "Okay, that definitely sounds call-back worthy."

We say good-bye, hang up, and then I lie in bed, staring up at the ceiling. It's quiet, and I'm guessing my mom went to work already, which means I have the house to myself until three, an hour after the bar closes, because she always spends an hour with whatever guy she's tempting to come home with her.

Boredom starts to set in. I hate being alone. It makes me feel even more invisible. If I had my way, I'd have someone around me all the time.

Finally, I can't take the silence anymore. I get out of bed, put on a pair of sweatpants and a tank top, pull my hair up and grab my classical music record from the stack of records on the floor. Moving to the record player on my bureau, I place the needle on it and Beethoven's *Moonlight* Sonata comes on.

I start to dance, letting the music own me as I picture myself on stage and everyone is watching. Fouetté en tournant. Grand jeté. Pirouette. My movements are slow, but graceful and powerful. Each brush of my toe, each twirl, each leg lift perfectly flowing with the music. I create a story simply by using my body, one of a girl who is not necessarily sad, but searching for something—she just doesn't know what it is yet.

The longer the song goes on, the more into it I get. The more overpowering the story becomes. I transform into someone else. Someone alive. Someone noticed. Someone not overlooked. I can picture myself on the stage dressed in tulle and feathers, starring as Odette in *Swan Lake*, and everyone sees me. Notices me. Is in awe.

By the time I'm finished, I'm almost in tears and I don't know why. I don't feel sad. In fact, I feel content.

I wish I could go back and savor the moment, realize just how amazing it was that I could feel that happy. It was the last summer I ever felt like that. Danced like that. Felt content. Eventually, I'd lose the will to do it anymore, and my pointe shoes would go in a box along with my Barbie phone and my *Flashdance* poster, everything that made up who I was at the start of the summer.

When I did dance again, it wouldn't be the same—I wouldn't be the same. Yes, I would cry, but not because I was moved. It would be because I was dancing topless on a stage in a front of a bunch of screaming strangers who wouldn't really see me, at least the real me who once dreamed of being Odette. To them I'd just be a plastic doll.

# Chapter 3

# She-Devil

Later that night, as I'm sitting in front of the television, debating whether I want to watch late-night reruns and keep folding laundry or go to bed, I hear the sound of music from next door. This isn't out of the ordinary. At least one of the houses in the neighborhood usually has a party during the weekend.

But this sounds like it's coming from next door, which doesn't really happen. Before Dylan's parents moved in, an elderly couple used to live there until they got sick of the noise and headed to Florida. And I rarely hear anything from Dylan's parents, except for maybe yelling.

Not wanting to be a stalker again, I try to resist the urge to look outside. But eventually it becomes too much, and I get up from the couch and pad over to the window. The driveway is packed with cars, along with the front of the house, and people are standing outside, laughing and smoking and drinking out of plastic cups. It's a full-blown party, topped off with a guy dancing in the front yard, high off his ass, and a blond girl wearing a leather dress, shaking her hips to the beat of the music on top of a car.

I'm about to look away, figuring I'll take Bryant's advice and steer away from any potential self-destructive behavior, when Dylan appears beside the guy smoking the joint. Dylan says something that makes the guy laugh, then he offers him the joint. He takes the joint and puts it up to his lips, inhaling slowly and deeply. I'm completely mesmerized watching his lips, the way he presses them tightly together when he pulls the joint out of his mouth. When he releases the smoke from his lungs, his tongue slips out and he licks lips.

I wish I was the one licking his lips. If I were my mother, I'd get out of my sweats and go over there. Put on a leather dress like the girl on the car and laugh and touch his arm until he came home with me.

But I'm not my mother.

I'm just Delilah.

So instead I just stare out the window, a little longer than I should, and he ends up glancing up at me. Because I left the light on in the kitchen, it lights the house just enough that he can see me.

I contemplate whether to duck and hide and prove that I'm a stalker, or just wave and shrug it off. *What would Poison Ivy do?* I lift my hand and wave at him, mustering up the best half smile that I can, then I start to turn around, but he holds up his finger like he wants me to wait. I pause as he hands the joint to the lanky guy then hops over the fence into my yard. He keeps his eyes on me as he makes his way up the sidewalk to my front steps, only looking away when he gets close enough to the front door that he can't see me anymore.

I back off the couch as he knocks and quickly run over to the laundry basket on the couch, rummaging through until I find a pair of my shorts and put them on. Then I tug the elastic out of my hair, shaking it out a little bit before running my fingers through it.

I move so fast that I have to catch my breath before I answer the door and forget to mentally prepare myself. When I catch sight of him, my heart slams so hard in my chest it actually hurts, and I almost fall to the floor, my knees shaking. I'm pretty sure he notices my reaction, but if he does, he doesn't say anything.

"Hey," he says, crossing his arms and leaning against the railing, looking all relaxed and sexy in his jeans and pinstriped shirt, the sleeves pushed up so I can see his tattoos and lean arms. "What are you doing?"

"Watching TV and folding laundry," I say, not realizing how lame it sounds until it actually leaves my mouth.

His lips quirk. "Sounds like a night full of possibilities."

I try to make a joke and salvage the start of a conversation. "If by possibilities you mean staying up and watching Jay Leno crack jokes while I binge on popcorn, then yeah, the possibilities are endless." I try to mimic the smile my mom makes every time she's trying to be cute. "In fact, I might even get really daring and stay up past midnight."

"Wow, staying up past midnight," he says, pressing his hand against his chest. "How very adventurous of you."

"What can I say. I like to live life on the wild side."

"I bet you do." His gaze flickers up and down my body and I feel something inside me lift. Then he glances over my shoulder and asks, "Is your mom home?"

My expression falters, and whatever was inside me that was lifting crashes. But as if he senses my disappointment, he adds, "I was just wondering if you were good to come over to the party, or if the parental was going to get in the way."

I love that he calls her "the parental," not "my hot sexy sister"

or the many other things she's been called that in no way imply
that she's a mother.

"Actually, she's at work until three," I tell him, the lifting sensation rising again, and I feel like I'm about to float away into the
sunset.

He glances at the watch. "So you're good to hang for at least a
few hours, right?"

I nod, telling myself to settle down and not be a dork by getting overly excited. "Yep, I'm cool." It's so not cool to say you're
cool, but thankfully Dylan seems to find my dorkiness mildly
adorable.

He grins at me and then motions me to follow him as he steps
down the stairway. I shut the door behind me and follow him
down the sidewalk, staying just behind him until we reach the
fence. There he jumps over, and then gives me his hand to help me
over. I hesitate, staring at his hand, offered to me. Me.

Finally, I take his hand, slipping my fingers through his. The
contact of his skin is amazing, creates heat that's more powerful
than the hot summer air flowing around us. His touch is what
authors write about. What women dream about. What singers
sing about.

And even though I didn't know it at the time, the moment
he took my hand, he owned me, which would seem amazing,
except for owning someone and loving someone aren't the same
thing.

He doesn't let go of my hand after he helps me over the fence.
I think he must like holding it. Either that, or he's forgotten that
he has it. I don't say anything as I follow him across the small strip
of lawn on the other side of the fence until we reach the side of the
car where the girl is dancing. I realize I know her. Nikki, a girl I
go to school with. The way she moves is enthralling, and everyone

is watching her. It's not like she's the greatest dancer. In fact, I'm sure I'm better. But she's like my mother, drawing in attention as if she were casting a magic spell over everyone.

I only look away from her when Dylan takes the joint from the lanky guy's hand and takes a hit as he introduces me. "Landon, this is Delilah."

Up close and in the light from the porch, I can see his face, and I realize that I know him.

I say, "Yeah, I know. We go to school together."

He's stoned, eyes bloodshot and ringed with red, so it takes him a moment to place me. But eventually recognition clicks. "Oh yeah, you had Mr. Melson for fourth, right?"

"And you always sat at the back and got lectured for drawing and not taking notes," I say, feeling my pulse pound as Dylan grazes his finger along the inside of my wrist.

"And you always got in trouble for being late," Landon says with a small smile.

I try not to shudder as Dylan's finger makes his way up my forearm. I want to look at him, see what's in his eyes, but I'm almost afraid to look. "What can I say," I tell Landon, tensing when Dylan hands me the joint. "I like to make an entrance." I stare down at the joint in my hand. *What the hell am I supposed to do with this?*

I've never smoked pot before and I think about just handing it back, but everyone's looking at me, waiting for me to take a hit— Dylan is waiting for me to take a hit. I don't want to disappoint him, so I put it up to my lips and inhale just like I saw him do earlier.

But the smoke stings and unable to hold it in, I let out a sharp choking cough that makes me feel ridiculous, especially when a few people laugh at me. Dylan doesn't, though. As I'm hacking my lungs out, Dylan takes the joint from my hand and gives it back to Landon. Then he swings his arm around my shoulder and pulls me closer to him, kissing the side of my head.

I no longer feel ridiculous.

In fact, I feel like the exact opposite.

I feel like Odette.

And he is Prince Siegfried.

I look up at him and he smiles down at me, moving me with him as he steps forward. "Come on, gorgeous, let's go get you a drink."

A smile spreads across my face as I walk with him, squeezing past two cars in the driveway and onto the front yard. He takes me inside his house that's full of people dancing and drinking.

"It's my birthday," he shouts over the music.

"Well, happy birthday then," I shout back, and he smiles again at me.

As we make our way through his house, I find myself noticing how much his eyes light up when he talks and how much they darken when he looks at me, not in a bad way, but in an I-notice-you way. It makes me happy and nervous at the same time, because no one has ever looked at me like that. By the time we reach the kitchen, I'm sweating and jittery inside, so when he hands me the drink, I devour it, hoping to calm my nerves. But it's vodka, and I choke on the fiery burn of it.

"Shit." I cough, throwing the plastic cup like it's made of poison.

He kicks the cup out of the way and steps closer to me, restraining a grin as he pats me on the back. "Are you okay?"

I nod, biting back a gag. "Super." I cough, pressing my hand to my chest as I stand back up. "I'm sorry. I thought it was water."

"Do you want me to get you a water so you can wash it down?"

he asks, watching me, his eyes always locked on me, unlike a lot of people who usually look through me when they talk to me, like I barely exist. At least that's what it feels like.

I shake my head. "No, I'm good now. I promise."

He nods and then scoots a few liquor bottles out of the way so he can hop on the counter, where he sits and lets his legs dangle over the edge. "So, other than dancing down the driveway and staying up all night and getting freaky with your laundry, what else do you like to do?" He flashes me a grin, and I nearly melt into a puddle right there on the kitchen floor for the crowd to tramp through.

"That's about it, really," I admit, scooting closer to him as people pack their way into the already crowded kitchen. "I'm actually pretty boring."

"I doubt that." His eyes fill with want. "In fact, aren't redheads supposed to be wild and fun?"

I self-consciously touch my hair, wishing that were true, wishing I could say yes, wishing I could be that for him. "I think that's blondes."

He shakes his hand, his gaze devouring me. "No way. It's definitely redheads." He considers something. "Blondes are known for being airheads."

I snort a laugh. "Well, my mom's a blonde, and she's no spacier than I am."

He considers something for a moment. "Your mom's a beautiful woman," he says, and it feels like a knife has entered my chest. He leans forward and touches the side of my head with his fingers. "You look just like her except for the hair."

"Thanks," I say, a little confused. "Wait, that was a compliment, right?"

He laughs as he hops off the counter. "It was, but since that wasn't completely clear, here's another one for you." He inches toward me, and I have to tip my head up to meet his eyes. Even though there are people around us, it feels like we're the only ones in the room.

We stand there for an eternity. He's eyeing my lips, and I'm struggling to breathe. Then I stop breathing altogether as he reaches forward and grazes his thumb across my bottom lip. "You have the most beautiful lips I've ever seen."

I want to say thank you, but I'm speechless, and the feeling only amplifies when he leans in like he's going to kiss me. But that can't be right, because gorgeous guys never want to kiss me.

But he does. It's just a slight brush of our lips, but it's enough for fireworks to shoot off inside my body. Enough for me to crumble into his arms. I lose myself in that kiss, and when he pulls away he takes a piece of me with him, one I'll never get back.

With his attention focused solely on me, he licks his lips with his tongue like he's savoring the aftertaste of me, then he takes my hand.

"You promised you'd dance for me." Then he leads me to the living room as the song switches to a slow one, but with a deafening bass that vibrates the windows. Everyone starts dancing, and it makes it hard for him to get us to the center of the living room, but eventually we make it.

Then he watches me, expecting me to dance just for him. And I want to give it to him, be the swan and mesmerize him, especially with how he's looking at me. But there are so many people around and not enough room and I'm a little nervous.

"You want me to dance for you here?" I ask, folding my arms across my chest.

He nods. "I do."

I glance around at the crowd. "I'm not sure if I can do that here."

Something flickers in his eyes, something I've never seen before, and it makes me hug myself tighter. "You're not going to dance for me?" he asks.

"I want to," I say quickly. "But there's not enough room." I inch toward him. "A rain check, though."

For a brief instant I think he's going to reject me, but then he smiles again. "You owe me a dance still." Then he grabs hold of my waist and pulls me to him. I hook my arms around his neck, feeling myself smile. Then we move to the beat, our eyes fixed on each other, our bodies aligned perfectly. Even though there are a lot of people grinding to the music and moving around us, no one seems to touch us. It's like we're protected by this bubble, and I feel powerful, no longer invisible but standing in the spotlight. He makes me feel that way just by looking at me, like I'm not just Delilah, but someone else. Someone who deserves to be standing center stage.

That's how we remain until the next song, moving to the rhythm, our bubble around us, eyes glued to each other, the crowd vanishing the closer we get.

Dylan leans in and his breath touches my cheek as he asks, "So on a scale of one to ten, how lame is this party?"

I slant back to look him in the eyes, but keep my hands on his shoulders, making sure I don't put too much room between us. "It's not lame at all. In fact, it's pretty fun."

He wavers, like he doesn't agree. "It's not the best one I've put together. In fact, in Alpine, I was known for my parties."

"You lived in Alpine before this?" I ask and he nods. "What did you do there besides throw parties?"

He studies me closely. "I'm not sure I can trust you with that answer yet."

"Why? Is it like a secret or something?" I ask.

He wavers again. "Or something."

I'm not sure how to respond. "Well, what do you do now, or is that a secret, too?"

He looks annoyed by my persistent questioning, but it swiftly vanishes as he says, "I'll tell you what. The next time we hang out together, on a real date, I'll tell you some of my secrets, Delilah Peirce."

At the time, I felt so happy about what he said, as if he cared enough about me to tell me his secrets, as if I had some sort of power over him. But if I had looked closer, hadn't been so blinded by the need to be seen, I would have seen that he had the control.

But I didn't see it like that and just kept dancing with him in a daze, engrossed by everything he did or said, like his looks and words were made of gold—maybe even worth more, because he made me feel like I was worth more.

Then Nikki showed up wearing her black leather dress that reminded me a lot of the black-feathered costume Odile wore in Swan Lake.

"Mind if I cut in?" she asks, tightening her arms at her side to create more cleavage.

Dylan snubs her. "No thanks, Nikki. I'm already dancing with Delilah."

I smile sweetly at her and I nearly feel the burn of her death glare as she starts to back away. "Well, maybe later, then. After little Miss Sweet-and-Innocent goes to bed," she says without looking at me, putting me in my place like a true she-devil.

Still, he ignores her and keeps his hands on my hips, swaying us to the music, and she finally walks away. We continue to dance and talk about lighter things, like our favorite food, color, band, car. We do this for hours, and every time he smiles or laughs at something I say, I feel my stomach somersault and feel myself never wanting the night to end.

But it does, and by the time I have to go home, I feel like I'm floating. Dylan walks me to my door. He brushes his lips across mine. And then he stays there until I'm safely inside and lock the door.

It's a perfect night. Everything is so perfect and I dance my way back to my room, feeling as though I just got a leading part. But then I look out the window just before I go to bed and see Dylan standing in the driveway talking to the she-devil herself, laughing as she touches his arm and leans in to whisper something in his ear. I tell myself it doesn't mean anything, that it's just talking and friendly touching, but as I lay in bed, hurting and on the verge of crying, I realize that tonight meant everything to me.

And that was a dangerous way to think, because I was already letting myself drown in Dylan and there was so much farther to sink. So many more tears. Heartache. Disappointment.

Pain.

# Chapter 4

# Maneater

It takes me some time to let the whole Nikki thing go. It's not like I say anything to Dylan about it, but every time we talk, I can't help but wonder if he hooked up with her that night, if he looked at her like he looked at me. Made her feel special like he makes me feel every day.

We haven't gone on an official date yet, so I still don't know his secrets. I do start spending a lot of time out in the front yard, though. Dance class has ended for the summer, so there's not a lot of stuff to do. But I keep busy, reading out in the front yard, tanning out in the front yard, even going as far as mowing the lawn, just so I can watch Dylan work on his car, occasionally checking out his ass and anything else I can get my eyes on.

The amazing thing is, he always comes up and talks to me. Every day for two weeks straight. A lot of our conversations are centered around the car he's working on. Even though I have no interest in cars, I nod and pretend that I'm superinterested in everything he says, so he'll keep on talking to me and hopefully like me. He also asks me a lot of questions, like my likes and dislikes, where I'm from, what I do for fun. He doesn't try to kiss me again, though, and I find myself missing the touch of his lips and the feelings the kiss stirred inside me.

"There's no way that could be true," I say after a very long conversation about music and concerts as we stand beside the fence. "You really saw Unwritten Law play?"

He nods as he wipes his greasy hands on a rag. "Yeah, three years ago." He tosses the rag on the ground. "They're even better live."

I wipe the sweat from my forehead. I'd been mowing the lawn when he finally came out of the house, and so I'm sweaty and gross, but I didn't want to walk away, afraid I'd miss the chance to talk to him if I did. "I think most bands are," I say. "At least more powerful. Well, except for heavy metal bands, but I can't stand that music anyway."

He nods in agreement. "Yeah, that's probably my least favorite, too."

"It's such a shame that you still can't watch old rock bands play like Lynyrd Skynyrd," I say. "Now that would be something to see."

"You seriously listen to Lynyrd Skynyrd?" he asks, making his way back to the fence after collecting a bottle of water from the cooler beside the car.

I nod, tucking a strand of hair behind my ear. "Yeah, I listen to a lot of classic rock actually, but that might be because my mom's been branding it into my head since I was five."

He angles his head to the side as his gaze quickly skims to the front door of my house just behind me. "Your mom seems like an interesting woman," he says.

I try not to react, even though I want to shout at him that she's a true maneater. "Yeah, I guess."

He leans against the fence, the muscles of his lean arms

rippling as he crosses them on top of the metal post. "What does she do for a living?" he asks.

"She works at a bar," I reply agitated. "Why?"

He shrugs. "I don't know...I just see her coming and going with a lot of men."

"That's because she sleeps with a new one every day." It sort of just slips out, but I don't want to take it back. In fact, I'm hoping it repulses him.

He arches a brow at me, looking more interested than he did before, which means I epically failed. "Really?" He considers something for a moment and keeps glancing at my house like my mom's going to walk out in her underwear, which probably wouldn't be the first time.

I press my lips together, hating how interested he is in her. "Well, I'm sure if you hit on her, she'd probably sleep with you too," I say spitefully.

He glances at me with a questioning look on his face. "You think so?"

Anger simmers under my skin. "Maybe. She likes her guys young."

His gaze bores into me. "And you'd be okay with that?"

"If you slept with my mother?" I ask. "You can do whatever you want." I hate my mother right now. Hate that she's so pretty. Hate that she likes to sleep with guys more than she likes her daughter, because I know right now if Dylan hit on her, she'd snatch him up, use him, then spit him back out.

Which is exactly what I want to do, except for the spitting-out part. I'd want to keep him.

He stares at me for a few moments longer, and then his intense gaze softens as he almost looks pleased. "You want to go some-where with me?"

My jaw nearly drops. What the hell? How do we go from asking questions about my mother to asking me out on a date finally? Still, I say, "Where?"

He stands up straight, wiping the sweat from his forehead with the back of his hand. "Me and a couple of friends are going to go down to the fair in Jackson to ride the rides and hang out. I'm sure it's going to be pretty lame, but we could make it fun." He winks at me and grins, dimples appearing, and my heart skips a beat.

"Sure, that sounds fun," I say in a calm voice, despite my giddiness.

"Does it?" He bites back his amusement as he starts to walk back to his house. "Alright then, Red, I'll pick you up at eight."

My brows knit. "Red?"

He suppresses a grin as he steps back toward me and extends his arm. I stop breathing, terrified and excited as he hooks his finger around a strand of my hair. "Yeah, your hair." He ravels it around his finger, tightly, pulling on it just enough that it sort of makes my scalp sting. "Red is actually my favorite color...I plan on painting my car red and everything." He tugs on my hair a little bit harder, watching my reaction with fascination. "In fact, I think I'm going to call you that from now on."

I'm not sure I agree with his nickname for me, because I can't help but think of the Marvel comic book character Red Sonja, who was a redhead and an amazingly beautiful temptress who rocked a bikini, and none of that begins to describe me—well, except for my red hair.

He releases my hair and tucks his hands in the pockets of his loose-fitting jeans. "I'll pick you up at eight," he says, and then turns away and goes back to his tools scattered on the driveway in front of his car.

I watch him bend over, rubbing my head where he pulled on my hair, butterflies fluttering in my stomach. It has to be a date.

I'm going on my first date.

I'm practically bouncing as I enter the living room. My mom must notice my overly happy attitude, too, because she immediately gets this weird look when she glances up from painting her toenails on the sofa. "Maneater" by Hall & Oates is playing from the stereo, and there's some sort of soap opera on the television, but the volume is turned down.

"What do you look so happy about?" she asks as she brushes the nail polish across her toenail.

I flop down on the sofa that's across from the one she's sitting on, grab a pillow, and place it on my lap. "A guy asked me out."

She glances up at me. "You mean the one that's been the cause of you over-mowing my front lawn."

"I have no idea what you're talking about." I feign dumb, not because I'm afraid she'll tease me or tell me he's too old for me. But because I'm afraid she'll steal him.

"Sure you don't." She shakes her head, smiling as she twists the nail polish lid back on. "So he finally asked you out?"

"Yes," I tell her, hugging the pillow against my chest.

She muses over this. "He's quite the catch. I'm proud of you, Delilah." I feel this ping of pride as she says it, and the sun feels a little brighter, like I'm not standing in her shadow. Then she turns on the sofa, props her feet up on the coffee table in front of her, and pats the spot on the sofa next to her. "Come sit by me so we can talk."

I sigh, get up, and cross the room, sitting down beside her. "Please tell me you're not going to give me a sex talk, because I already know how that works."

She raises her eyebrows at me with curiosity. "How well do you know?"

For some reason, I feel ashamed as I admit the truth. "Not that well." My cheeks heat. "I mean, I'm still a virgin."

She looks me over, like she's trying to weigh if that fact has anything to do with my looks or not. I'm not sure what she decides, but when she looks away, she reaches for her purse on the table. She unzips it, reaches in, and takes something out. "Take this with you." She hands me what's in her hand.

I stare down at the condom. "Mom, I don't think—"

"You may not think anything's going to happen," she interrupts me. "But you're a beautiful girl, Delilah, and if you decide to use that beauty, I want to make sure you have control over the situation." She stands up and walks awkwardly toward the hallway because her toenails are still drying. "Don't ever leave it up to the guy to make decisions for you," she calls over her shoulder, exiting the room.

As much as I was jealous of my mother, she had an excellent point. One I wish I would have listened to on a deeper level, taken it as a subtle warning not just to protect myself from sex, but to protect myself from getting hurt, lost, losing myself.

It's funny, but it was one of the last real conversations we had that really meant anything. As the years went by we drifted, and when I left, she never came looking for me. I wonder if she'll ever find out that I died. Or when or if my body is discovered, I'll just end up as another insignificant and unidentified Jane Doe.

# Chapter 5

# The Red Dress

Dylan wasn't lying when he said he'd come pick me up. He actually walked over to my house, even though I was planning on wandering out to the front yard so we could just meet.

My mom's the one who answered the door, and I can hear her chatting away with him in the living room, laughing. The sound is heavy metal to my ears, and I hope she's wearing clothes, but I doubt it.

I'm trying to hurry and get ready. I was so nervous I couldn't figure out what to wear. At first I was going to go with something more along the lines of my normal wardrobe, like skinny jeans, sandals, and maybe a fancy tank top. But then I couldn't help but think of that busty blond girl named Nikki and the slutty leather dress she was wearing and how she captured everyone's attention when she was dancing on the car. So I decided on something a little less Delilah and a little more sexy and fitting for the nickname "Red."

"Heart of Glass" by Blondie is playing from my record player as I work to get my hair up into some kind of fancy 'do and dance around every once and awhile. But it's hot, and the stifling air is making my hair limp. I wanted to make it look really sexy since Dylan was playing with it, but I'm giving up hope the more it falls out of the clips. Finally I just pull all the strands out and run my fingers through them, so they're a little wavy. Then I stain my lips with some red lipstick I stole out of my mother's makeup stash. After adding a string of pearls to look more grown up, I go over to the full-length mirror and examine my reflection.

I'm wearing a red dress that hugs my body and a lacy push-up bra that's been sitting in my dresser since my mom gave it to me when I was fourteen—I even had to pull the tags off. But it's padded and has an underwire and makes my breasts swell out of the top of the neckline.

"I have cleavage," I say, turning to the side and sticking out my chest proudly as I run my hands all over my curves. My hair running down to my shoulders and the white pearls sort of clash with the sexy black heels, but it's only minor, and for once I actually like how I look.

Because I'm not bland.

Invisible.

I radiate like fire.

For the first time ever, I feel confident.

I feel like Red.

But then my mom walks into my room, wearing nothing but a silk shorts and matching tank top with no bra, and suddenly the illusion of the goddess in the mirror shatters.

"You look nice," she says, after opening the door.

"Thanks," I say, reaching for my perfume on the dresser. "Is Dylan out there waiting?"

She nods and then leaves the door open as she walks away. I take a deep breath, feeling my nerves shiver inside me, but keep my chin up as I grab my purse and head out to the living room.

When I enter, Dylan has his back turned to me as he looks at some of the photos on the wall of what used to be my family. I'm not sure how to get his attention, so I clear my throat.

He turns, and I clutch onto my purse as he scans over my outfit, my hair, my body. "You look amazing," he says with lust in his eyes that makes me glad I chose the red dress.

A slow, unsteady breath eases from my lips. "Thank you."

He glances over me again and more lust radiates from him. "You're welcome," he says, and then offers me his hand.

I take it and again I feel the magic in his touch as he leads me toward the door. I thought the night was so full magic and possibilities that I was going to change because of it.

And I did.

But not for the better.

# Chapter 6

# Red and the Big Bad Wolf

Summers in Maple Grove are surprisingly hot, considering how intense our winters are. It's eight thirty at night and it still feels as hot as it did midday. But I'm enjoying the heat as I wander around the fair with Dylan at my side, the smell of cotton candy and caramel apples in the air, the sounds of roller coasters and other rides in the background. Lights flashing everywhere. It's a magical night and I feel like Cinderella at the ball, especially with the way Dylan keeps looking at me and how he holds my hand for the entire world to see and doesn't let it go, even when a few of his friends join us for a while.

We spend a lot of time riding the rides, ones that he lets me pick, never complaining even when I say I want to ride the Ferris wheel, which is known as the "couples' ride." He tells me I look pretty, that he likes my laugh. He smiles a lot. He has a really nice smile, one that makes people turn their heads and makes me forget how to breathe.

By the time we're coming off the Tilt-A-Whirl, I'm high off the night, so elated I do a few pique turns when I'm going down the exit ramp with my arms out in front of me, spotting all the way to the bottom.

Dylan laughs as I reach the bottom. "That was impressive."

"That was nothing," I say proudly and then do a few fouetté turns, swinging my leg out as I spin in place on one toe. I smile when I finish and Dylan smiles back, completely entertained, and it makes me feel warm and breathless inside.

Then he steps off the exit ramp and brushes his hand across my lower back before heading toward the concessions. "So, Red." He's wearing a pair of dark jeans with a little bit of fray on them. His black shirt is just tight enough that I can see how solid his chest is. He's also got a black baseball cap on that he's wearing backward, hiding his hair, but he still looks as sexy as he does standing out shirtless working on his car. "Tell me something about yourself."

"Like what?" I ask, fiddling with the strap on my dress, my skin damp from the heat and doing the dance moves.

He shrugs. "Anything," he says. "Who you are? Where you're from? I want to learn more about you."

I fan my hand in front of my face. "Well, I actually used to live in Fairmount, but then my mom and dad got divorced a few years ago and we moved here because my mom needed to start over."

"Do you ever go visit your dad?" he asks, watching me as we walk, the lights around us reflecting in his eyes.

I shake my head. "I haven't seen him since the divorce."

He gives me a sympathetic look. "That sucks."

I nod in agreement, staring at a candy apple booth beside me. "Yeah, but it's probably for the best."

There's a brief pause, and when I glance over at him, he's giving me a quizzical look. "How do you figure?" he asks.

I shrug, stopping and shuffling my heels against the dirt.

"Well, he wanted a do-over too, like my mom, only instead of relocating he got a perfect new family, and I don't really fit into that picture."

His eyes leisurely scan over my legs, my cleavage, my neck, finally landing on my eyes. His eyes are hooded and gorgeous and his attention makes me feel special. "You look pretty perfect to me."

My cheeks heat from his compliment. No guy has ever talked to me like this, and I feel like I'm going to melt. "Thanks, but I don't think he agrees," I say, and we start to walk again. "In fact, he made that pretty clear when he signed over full custody to my mom because he"—I make air quotes—"didn't have time to raise a teenager the right way." I lower my hands to my sides. "Whatever the hell that means."

"I think your dad is an asshole," he says with so much anger in his voice it startles me a little. And it should have startled me more. I wish I could go back and shake that girl, tell her to wake up and see the signs, but I can't. All I can do is remember.

He reaches out and cups my cheek. The anger still there, and I can feel his hand trembling. "How could he not want you?"

His words are so overwhelming I start to tremble, fighting to keep my legs under me. He can feel it, too, and he brings his other hand up and cups my face between his hands.

"Hey, you want to go somewhere more private?" he asks, a slow smile spreading across his face. "Somewhere where we could talk some more without all the noise and chaos."

I nod eagerly. "Yeah, I'd really like that."

\* \* \*

He takes me up to Star Lookout, where teenagers are known to go and make out. I've never been there, but once we get up there

I realize the allure of the place. It's got a gorgeous view of the city, the lights sparkling below and the stars twinkling from above. Plus it's quiet and there's no one around, so we have a lot of privacy.

"You know, I used to come up here a lot in high school," he admits after we park and he puts the parking brake on, leaving the air conditioning on and the radio, along with the headlights.

I want to ask him if he's brought other girls up here, but not wanting to seem absurdly jealous, I ask, "Wasn't that, like, this year?"

He shakes his head. "I haven't been to school in two years." He pauses, watching me. "I dropped out at the beginning of my junior year."

"Oh." I'm not sure how to respond.

"Do you think less of me now?" he asks, more entertained by my uncomfortable reaction than anything. "That you're on a date with a high school dropout?"

"Not really." I turn in my seat and face him, tucking my dress under my legs. "I'm not that great in school myself."

"Yeah, but you still go," he says, rotating in his seat and leaning against the door, his attention still fixed on me. "I chose to give up and be a deadbeat."

"You're not a deadbeat," I tell him. "You work."

"Yeah, but I don't have a steady job," he says, bitterness slipping into his voice for a brief moment. "I'm just a washed-up loser at eighteen."

My heart aches for him. "I don't believe that's true at all."

"Yeah, but you barely even know me. And if you asked my father, he'd tell you how wrong you are."

"Well, I think your father's an idiot. In fact, most are."

He sits quietly in the dark for a moment, and when he speaks again he sounds calm and content. "You think so?"

I nod, loving that I made him feel better. "I know so."

He scoots closer to me and leans forward toward the console. "You know what, Red, you are very wise for a sixteen-year-old."

My expression immediately falls. "I'm seventeen."

He reaches for me and grabs a lock of my hair. "I think it's cute that you're trying to pretend you're older," he says. "But I promise it doesn't matter." He plays with the strand of my hair, tugging on it. "And word of advice. The next time you lie about your age, you should let your mom in on it."

"She told you." I frown, feeling ridiculous.

He chuckles lowly. "She actually told me a lot."

"Like what?"

He starts twisting my hair around his finger, forcing my head closer to him, almost like he's reeling me into him. "Lots and lots of stuff, like how you've never had a boyfriend before," he says, seeming pleased. "But let's not talk about that."

Then, giving me no time to get embarrassed, he tugs on my hair just a little bit and my lips crash into his. The taste of him soars through me. I feel high. Powerful. Intoxicated. And the sensation only builds when he pulls me over the seat and onto his lap so I'm straddling him, and he does it somehow without breaking the kiss.

At first everything starts off innocently. Our tongues gently searching each other's mouth, him playing with my hair and running his fingers along my shoulders. He even shudders once when I bite gently on his bottom lip, something I saw a woman do on television once.

Then his hand starts to wander under my dress, inching under the fabric. And the more heated our kiss gets, the higher his palm slides up, until finally he's cupping my ass.

I've never done this with a guy before, and I feel breathless and excited and terrified all at the same time, because it's new and I'm not one hundred percent sure that I should want him to touch me this way as much as I do.

I'm so confused, and my confusion only increases when he leans back, gripping the bottom of my dress, and tugs it over my head, without even giving me time to react. But he looks really distracted right now as he tosses the dress aside, his eyes drinking my body in.

I'm still afraid, although the longer he looks at me with desire burning in his eyes, the more relaxed I get. But as he reaches for the clasp of my bra, I panic.

"I've never done this before," I sputter, crossing my arms across my chest.

His eyes slowly slide up from cleavage to my eyes. "I sort of guessed that," he says, placing a hand on my cheek and wetting his lips with his tongue.

I feel transparent, no longer special, like how I felt at the carnival. "I'm sorry."

"It's okay," he says, briefly searching my eyes. "The first time can be scary, but I promise it'll be worth it."

I swallow hard, because I'm not sure I want my first time to be right now. I try to figure out the best way to tell him that as he reaches around and unhooks my bra, but I'm conflicted between wanting him to keep touching me and looking at me like this and wanting him to stop.

"God, you're beautiful," he says as the bra falls from my body and my breasts are exposed. He reaches out and brushes his finger across my nipple with this hunger in his eyes, and I gasp. The noise seems to turn him on more, the hunger darkening and taking over everything about him, from the way he moves to the ragged intake of his breath, and it makes me feel powerful for a moment. "I just want to kiss you all over." He keeps touching my breast as he leans forward to kiss me, and my stomach spins with emotions. "I promise this will be good," he says with his lips hovering over mine.

"But what if I can't," I whisper, hating myself at the moment for not being more confident, for not being able to be like my mother and own the moment.

"You can," he says. "I'll take care of you."

I don't want to make him mad, but at the same time I'm terrified out of my damn mind. "But I'm not sure I'm ready," I say, feeling the slightest bit of weight lifted off my shoulders until he leans back a little and looks at me and that intense emotion in his eyes looks like it's about to burst out.

He's angry with me and is no longer looking at me like he wants me. I can feel myself disappearing, vanishing back into Delilah. Becoming Invisible Woman again.

"Maybe I should just take you home," he says, leaning away and looking out the window, not at me.

My mind is racing, and I keep feeling myself fading the longer he looks away from me. And then he starts to move me away and I open my lips to protest, but all that comes out is, "Wait, I want to do this."

I'm not sure if it's the right thing to say, but he looks at me and I feel the slightest bit better. Yet for some reason my shoulders feel more weighted as the pressure builds inside me.

"Are you sure?" he asks, leaning closer, his eyes focused on my chest.

I give a very shaky nod, my whole body trembling. Then he looks up at me and the lust in his eyes is so overwhelming I have to shut my own eyes. Seconds later, he kisses me and I kiss him back, letting his hands wander all over my body, feeling my skin, touching me. The longer he feels me the more settled I get. I don't feel as nervous. As scared. And when he lays me down on the backseat of the car and looks down at me, I literally become lost in him.

I'll spare you the details of the rest, other than we had sex, it hurt, and he held me afterwards. That was probably the only part I liked about that night; lying in the backseat of his car with my head resting on his chest, my thoughts racing a million miles a minute.

Even looking back at it now, I still get confused over what was going on in my head that night. Why I couldn't see it for what it was. Why I couldn't be stronger and tell him that I wasn't ready. Why I couldn't just do what I wanted to do, instead of what he wanted to. Why I couldn't see that I wasn't Odette and he wasn't Prince Siegfried. That instead I was Little Red Riding Hood and he was the Big Bad Wolf.

## Chapter 7

# The Thunder Before the Rain

It's funny how when I look back on my life, I can see all the mistakes I made and how blinded I was by wanting to be noticed. I'd spent so many years in my mother's shadow that when a guy finally noticed me, I thought it made me stronger. But really, it only made me weaker.

Maybe if I knew what lay ahead of me, I'd have wanted to stay in the shadows and remain unnoticed. But honestly, I doubt it. I think I was too vain at the time to believe that anything could happen to me, especially death.

And now all I can do is lie here in the cold water, staring up at the storm clouds, listening to my heartbeat fade away, and reflect on how I lived my life...let my memories take me over and haunt me...

Despite my awkward and uncomfortable first time, I end up having sex with Dylan a lot. By mid-July, we are one hundred percent consumed by each other, spending every waking hour together. We go to parties, and instead of hanging out in my front yard, watching him work on his car, I sit in a folding up chair beside the car while we talk.

Not to say that everything is perfect. Sometimes we argue over stuff, like what we're going to do for the night. It's nothing major and we make things work. Plus, he always makes me feel special. Always holds my hand. Always kisses me. Touches me. Always lets everyone know I'm his.

I've pretty much been walking around with a huge smile on my face for weeks now, something my mom's noticed.

"God, I forgot how exciting everything is when you're young," she comments as I enter the kitchen wearing the red dress, because I love how Dylan looks at me whenever I wear it.

I grab a bottle of water from the fridge and skip toward the doorway, doing a little pirouette. "Aw, to be young again," I joke, and part of me loves that she's looking at me with a hint of jealousy instead of the other way around. That I don't feel so insignificant standing in the same room as her when she's wearing nothing but a nighty.

"So where are you going tonight?" she asks as she takes out a pan to cook dinner.

I check my reflection in the small mirror on the wall. "To a party."

She sets the pan down on the stove. "You're being careful, right?"

I nod. "Always."

She turns up the temperature of the burner. "Good."

I leave the room and go get my purse before heading out to meet Dylan. It's nearing sundown and storm clouds are rolling in. I hear a boom in the distance, the thunder before the rain, and I step back inside and grab my jacket off the coatrack. I slip it on as I cross the lawn and wind around the fence to Dylan's driveway. Then I sit on the hood of his car and wait for him to come out, because he told me never to knock on the door, that his mother hates when people come over.

But twenty minutes go by and he still hasn't come outside. I eye the door, willing him to come out, but it stays shut. The sky starts to rumble again. Lightning strikes and flashes across the land. And then the rain comes pouring down.

I jump up from the car and run up to his front door, soaked by the time I get there. I hesitate before I knock quietly. No one answers, so I knock a little harder, then I startle back when it swings open. Dylan stands there with more anger in his eyes than I've ever seen, and it's all directed at me.

"I thought I told you to never knock on the damn door," he growls, his chest heaving with his breaths.

I trip backward and into the rain. "I'm sorry."

His mom starts shouting in the background, telling him to shut the damn door, that he's in deep shit for making noise and waking up his father. That he's such a fuckup. With each one of her words, he gets tenser. Angrier. But he doesn't say anything back. He just bottles it in and steps outside, slamming the door behind.

He doesn't say a word to me as he brushes by me, stomps through the puddles to his car, and climbs in. I stand on the porch in the rain, my jacket drenched, wondering if I should follow him. He seems so angry that I'm not sure what to do. But he keeps sitting in his car with the engine running, like he's waiting for me, so finally I run to the car and hop into the passenger seat.

His knuckles are white as he grips the steering wheel, breathing in and out. He's not wearing a jacket, his T-shirt is soaked, and beads of rain roll over his skin.

"Are you okay?" I ask, wiping some of the rain off my forehead.

He doesn't look at me. "I'm fine," he says coldly, and then he puts the car into reverse and backs into the road.

He doesn't speak as he drives down the street toward the edge of town. The longer the silence goes on, the smaller I feel. I watch the buildings and houses blur by, the rain crashing down against the ground and washing everything away.

"I'm sorry I knocked on the door," I finally tell him as he turns off the main street and down a dirt road where trees line the side and mountains are in the distance.

"It doesn't matter if you're sorry," he says, his attention straight ahead on the road. I can see the lightning reflect in his eyes every time it snaps, and it lights up his anger.

I start to grow nervous. "Where are we going? Is the party up here or something?"

He doesn't answer me and a few minutes later he stops the car at a turnout beneath a canopy of tree branches. I look around, wondering why we're here, wondering why he won't look at me. Wondering if he'll ever look at me again.

Without saying a word, he turns off the engine, gets out of the car, and stands in the rain in front of the car. I watch him lower his head, the rain pounding down on him, making him sink lower, like he's drowning.

Finally I get out of the car and take tentative steps toward him, the ground below me soft, and my sandals sink into it. When I reach him, he doesn't look up at me right away. He stares at the ground, a thin trail of water trickling off his forehead. The longer the silence goes on, the more I wish he would look at me. *Please.* I can't take the silence anymore. The invisibility.

Eventually, he gives me what I want without asking, elevating his chin, and his eyes lock with mine. Part of me wishes I could take back my inner wish, that I could tell him to look at the ground, because he's looking at me like he hates me.

"Do you know what you've done?" he asks, stepping forward.

"How much I'm going to deal with for you knocking on that damn door?"

"I said I was sorry," I tell him in a shaky voice. "But you weren't coming out, and I don't know another way to get a hold of you."

My excuses make him angrier, his face reddening. "Then you should have just waited by the car like I told you."

"But it was raining," I say, wrapping my arms around me as the cold seeps into my bones. "And I got cold."

"Cold." He gapes at me, fury burning in his eyes as thunder and lightning snap above us. "You've made the next week of my life a living hell because you were cold." He lets out this sharp laugh, but not because he thinks it's funny. He starts pacing in front of the car, running his fingers through his wet hair, clenching his hands into fists. "Do you know what it's like? To be yelled at all the time?" He pauses, like he's waiting for me to answer, and I shake my head. "Of course you don't." He laughs again, and it's filled with so much pain and anger that it makes my hairs stand on end. "I should have never got involved with you," he says. "You were too immature. I knew it, yet I looked past it because I wanted you." He turns away from me and starts walking toward the trees, like he's going to disappear into the forest and leave me alone. "God, you can't even listen to a simple direction."

I panic the further he gets from me, not wanting to be alone, and ultimately I rush after him. "Dylan, I'm sorry," I say. "I promise, I'll make it better. Tell me what I can do to make it better." I catch up with him and wrap my fingers around his arm, trying to pull him back to me.

As soon as I touch him, I feel this ripple course through his body. I don't even realize what's happening until it's over. Until his fist collides with my cheek. Until my ears start to ring. Until the world spins. Until the pain sets in.

I cup my aching cheek as he stands in front of me, looking so much calmer as hot tears spill down my cheeks and the raindrops instantly wash them away.

When I replay the moment in my mind, I can see how my pain brought him some sort of peace from his own internal pain, pain that I would never fully begin to understand. But at the time, I didn't see it. At the time, I only felt my own pain and shame. My own worry that this meant it was all over.

That I was no longer Odette.

The swan.

That I would become Delilah again.

It seemed so repulsive. So horrifying. To become that girl again. The one no one saw. The one that lived in the shadows.

God, what I would give to be that girl again.

## Chapter 8

# The Death of Delilah and the Making of Red

Over the next couple of days, I keep my distance from Dylan, and he seems to be keeping his distance from me. I see him working on his car sometimes, but I don't dare go out, afraid of what he'll say to me, afraid he'll hit me again, afraid he'll say that's it's really over, that he never wants to see me again.

I'd like to tell you that part of the reason I kept my distance was because I was mad at him for hitting me, but sadly that wasn't the case. Anger over that never crossed my mind. Only fear. I was so afraid of being alone again that it consumed my mind.

The fear only grew whenever I'd spend time in the kitchen, eating breakfast with my mom and her latest one-night stand.

"Your cheek looks like it's healing," my mom notes as she pours syrup onto a stack of pancakes. It's the fifth morning in a row I've eaten breakfast with her and a different guy.

I touch my cheek, remembering the snap of lightning before the strike, remembering how Dylan dropped me off at home without saying a word, and how when my mother asked me what happened, I said a got into a fight with a girl at a party. "It still hurts, though," I say.

"Well, maybe you should walk away from the fight next time," she says, cutting her pancakes with her fork.

Her twentysomething-year-old with a goatee looks up from his pancakes. "Why? Girl fights are hot."

She smiles at him, this haunting smile, and I'm pretty sure he catches his breath. It annoys me the way that he's looking at her, and I want him to stop it. I want him to look at me.

"I get into them all the time," I say, trying to get him to look away from my mother.

He doesn't. In fact, he leans in and kisses her. A few touches and groans later, they're in my mother's room and music is playing. And again I've become Invisible Girl, sitting in the shadows of the kitchen, the quiet wrapped around me.

I eat my pancakes, taking my time, knowing that when I'm done I'm going to have nothing else to do. I'm swallowing my last bite when I hear a knock on the door. I get up and make my way over to the door, sadness overpowering me. I no longer feel like Odette. Not even a swan. My wings are gone, and all the magic that Dylan created is dead, and I feel like I died right along with it.

Then I open the door, and he's standing there with a single rose in his hand. His eyes are on me, remorse on his face, pain and sadness in shadowing his eyes.

"I'm sorry," he says with agony in his voice. His gaze locks on my cheek, where a bit of red still remains. "I was just so upset and I…God, I'm such an asshole, hitting you like that." He pauses, like he's waiting for me to say something, but I can't find my voice. So he steps closer into the doorway and I don't step back. "I was just upset…my mom was yelling at me all morning and it just made me so angry…it always does." He swallows hard. "I promise, I'll never hurt you again. I swear to God, if you give me another chance…" He dares to touch my face and holds my cheek in his palm. "Please tell me you'll give me another chance."

As his words crash into me, so does the music from my mother's room. They both overwhelm me, one washing me away, one giving me back the light I so desperately want. I'm not even sure if I fully believe him, yet I tell myself I do as I nod.

"I forgive you," I say.

He smiles, leaning in to kiss me, and I kiss him back, let his kiss consume me and make everything feel better.

One might look at it as the point at which my fall started, where I made the wrong choice that would lead to five years of wrong choices that ultimately would lead to my half-beaten body being left for dead near the riverbank, reflecting on my life instead of living it.

But I don't believe it was.

I believe I started falling the moment I put on that red dress; the moment I stopped being who I really was. The moment I changed for someone else simply because he noticed me.

The moment I stopped being Delilah and I became Red.

*Tristan: Finding Hope*

# *Prologue*

*19 years old…*

I think I've finally become invisible. That I've somehow faded into a ghost just like I pretended to do when I was a kid. It was number two on my list of superpowers I wanted to have, right before X-ray vision—mainly because I wished I could see through Tina Bellonte's shirt—and right after wishing how to fly. I'm pretty sure the invisibility parts came true. X-ray vision got scratched off because I can see underneath women's shirts now pretty much whenever I feel like it. And flying…well, I'm fairly sure I know how to fly right now. I swear to God I do. I just need to get the balls to test the theory. Take the last step.

"Tristan man, get down from there. You're fucking tripping," Dylan calls out from three stories down where the bottom of the apartment reaches the concrete, proving that I might have been wrong about the invisibility because apparently he can see me. But then again, being seen by Dylan isn't that great of a thing. I wouldn't necessarily call him a friend, but probably as close as I've ever got to having one. He doesn't talk much, doesn't ask me questions about my life, which I like. Although he is kind of a douche, but hey, aren't we all at some point.

"Leave me alone," I holler back, the night sky above me, so far away, yet when I reach my hand up, it feels like I'm touching the stars.

"Not until your dumb ass gets down," he shouts, then takes a swig of his beer.

I shake my head, cigarette resting between my lips, arms outstretched to my sides, the wind in my hair. One more step and my flying theory will be tested. "No way. Not unless I jump. It's the only way."

"To what?"

"To see if I can fly."

Dylan shakes his head. "Not that shit again. Jesus, you do this every time you hit acid, man." He chucks the beer bottle out into the parking lot, annoyed.

"I'm not even that high anymore." Sadly, it's the truth. I'm up here of my own free will. Because I was sitting in a room full of people, laughing, drinking, doing drugs, and I was just there, existent, but nonexistent at the same time. It's been that way forever, me just living life in the shadows while everyone else seems to be in the sunlight.

"Tristan, the last thing anyone needs here is for the police to show up because your dumb ass couldn't handle his high and decided to try and kill himself," Dylan says, getting really pissed off now.

"That's not what I'm doing." I stare straight ahead at the trees across the street. I'm not lying either. I don't have a death wish. I'm just confused and trying to sort stuff out, trying to find a point to all of this. Life. It confuses the hell out of me. People, they confuse the hell out of me. Hell, I confuse the hell out of myself.

I've been confused for years, the feeling only amplifying the day my parents found out my sister, Ryder, died in a car accident. A car accident where my cousin, Quinton, was driving and crashed into another car—not his fault, just a freak accident. My parents blame him for it though and have been focusing all their energy on making sure to hate him every single day of his life since it happened. They've been telling me to do the same, but I've never been one to hold grudges. It takes too much energy that I don't have. So when Quinton called me up, asking for a place to crash this summer, I said okay without much hesitation. Granted I was fucking stoned out of my mind, but still, I'm sure I would have done it sober too. Besides, from what I've heard through the family grapevine, Quinton's been paying for what happened through his own depressing, drug-induced life. So why should I add to his misery?

When I told my parents he was staying with me, though, I officially got shunned by the family. I've been shunned by the family a total of nineteen times or so. It's nothing new. Being alone is nothing new. I'm sure eventually they'll talk to me again and I'll let it all go, because that's what I do. I'm not even sure why I care to have them in my life. They've barely acknowledged me ever since I turned sixteen and started getting into trouble, doing drugs for no other reason than I felt lost in life and alone and drugs temporarily filled that void. I couldn't find a purpose in anything. Couldn't find friends. But drugs numbed the confusion and made the people around me doing the same thing relatable enough that I could pretend I had friends. When I'm stoned, I'm not so alone, or at least I can see it that way.

This has been my life for the last few years. Getting stoned, drunk, trashed, and each time I got busted, my parents ignored me even more. I became more invisible. After Ryder died, it only got worse. She was "the good one," according to them. And maybe she was. She did well in school while I wasted my "intelligent mind." She didn't get arrested for being a minor under the influence and get put on probation. Didn't move out of the house to live in a "shit-hole trailer park to deal drugs." And they're right. She was the good one. I'm the bad and I can't change it. I am who I am.

"I'm going to fucking do it this time," I yell to Dylan, taking a few massively deep breaths, psyching myself up as I inch my feet closer to the ledge. "I swear I am. And just watch. I'm going to make it."

"Come down and I'll get Mallory to fuck you," he entices.

"I don't want a pity fuck," I say. "I've had way too many of those."

Dylan shakes his head and then throws his arms in the air, exasperated. "Fine. Do whatever the hell you want. It's your funeral." Then he storms off toward the entrance to the apartment, leaving me alone. There's nothing stopping me from jumping off the ledge.

*Just move your feet. Do it! Stop being such a pussy and fly.*

I wonder if I fell off the roof, if anyone would see me. Or if maybe I'd just fly away to the stars, never to be seen again. I could do it and find out—I *should* do it and find out. But after standing there for what seems like hours, I realize it's not going to happen and I step back.

Instead of flying for the night, I settle on climbing down from the roof and going back into the house to take another hit. I hang out with people who don't see me. Sleep with a girl who doesn't know my name. Then I pass out, knowing that when I wake up tomorrow, I'll do the whole thing over again. This is my life. There is no meaning. And I wonder if this is how it'll always be. If I'll always feel so dead and disconnected inside. So alone.

So invisible.

# Chapter 1

*4 years later…*

$M$y life is one bumpy roller coaster. The last few years I've been getting high, getting sober. High. Sober. High. Sober. I've lost track of how many times I've gotten clean. I want to say I'll never do it again, but I'd be the biggest fucking liar on the planet. I'll probably do it again, because I struggle to find motivation not to do it and being sober just makes me focus on life. You'd think after spending years on a downward spiral, almost OD'ing, losing my sister, falling in love with a girl—Nova Reed—who ended up falling in love with my cousin—Quinton—getting hepatitis C and having to go through a bunch of treatment to get rid of it, that I'd finally point the finger to the drugs and say that they must be doing this all to me. Sometimes I can see it, how fucked up I am on them, and so I try to stop. But I still always fall back to them, the pull too strong, the need to block out too great. I'm an addict. Plain and simple.

Right now, I'm supposed to be a builder. I've been spending the last several months on the road working for Habitat for

Humanity. It's actually more Quinton's thing. Ever since he got sober, he's been all about helping the world. I think he thinks if he is always doing something good then it'll make up for the accident, which maybe that's the case. And I'm happy he found his sanctuary, the place that makes him feel whole without being jacked up on heroin and methamphetamine. I think Nova helps with that too—helps him stay clean.

Me, well I'm not that strong. I don't really have anyone but myself, which makes it easier to disappear and fall off the cliff again until someone convinces me to climb back up for a little bit. Which is why I'm here. Well, sort of. I was basically dragged into this because Quinton and Nova thought I needed a good distraction from my life of misdirection and bad choices. And they're probably right. I just wish I could focus more on the distraction instead of the addiction.

"Hey, hand me that nail gun, would you?" Quinton says while messing around with one of the cupboard doors. The house we're working on right now should be finished by tomorrow and then we'll be on the road again, to I think Georgia.

Quinton wipes some sweat from his brow as I reach down and pick up the nail gun beside my feet with the hand that's not holding the cigarette. I give it to him and he shoots a few nails in the side of the house. "I'm fucking hot." My shirt is soaked in sweat and sticking to my back. "When are we quitting today?"

Quinton sighs. I'm sure he's getting irritated with my lack of motivation. But he'll never say anything because of my sister. I think part of him will always blame himself for her death, and for some reason he thinks he needs to be nice to me even when I might not deserve it. "You can take off if you want to, but I think Nova had something planned for tonight." He puts the nail gun on the ground and picks up a bottle of water. "To celebrate you being hepatitis free and all."

I shake my head. I just found out yesterday at my doctor visit that I'm officially disease free again and I'm glad. "She knows it's not normal to celebrate something like that, right? It's not like I was cured of cancer or something." I grab my own bottle of water that's beside the cooler. "I got the disease because I was a fucking idiot and shared needles with a bunch of druggies."

He scratches the back of his neck, looking uncomfortable, then takes along sip of his water. "Look, man. I totally get the self-blame and everything." He raises his eyebrows as he puts the lid back on the water. "But trust me, just be grateful you're clean and healthy now. We can celebrate that, right?"

I want to point out how many times I've slipped up on the clean part—the last time being only three weeks ago, a day when I did a line of meth—but I decide to be cooperative since he's letting me bail on building early. "All right, I'm down for celebrating, but what I'd really like to do is get laid. It's been a long time."

Quinton rolls his eyes. "Only you."

I hold back a smile and shrug, start packing up my tools, thinking about how I'll go back to the hotel and sit there in the silence, wondering how long I'll let the empty feeling go on. Maybe I'll turn on some television, but not to really watch it. Just to hear the noise so I'll try not to think about all the hell I went through and how much I want to fall back into to it.

But in the end it's all I'll think about, no matter what I do.

# Chapter 2

It's always been a little awkward being around Nova Reed because we have some history together and now that she's with my cousin, it's just plain weird. I'm not even sure when I actually started liking her to begin with. I think it was around when I was eighteen and we had this really hot make-out session, or at least I thought we did until she started crying and then ran off. She was just always such a nice, good person and cute as hell and she saw me for some reason, although always as a friend. I've gotten to know her over the last few years and she really helped me out for a while after the first time I got clean. I managed to sneak in a few kisses here and there, but she never really reciprocated them. Then she fell in love with my cousin and I permanently went into the friend zone. Yeah, I'm that fucking cool. Seriously, it's the story of my life. I've never really been in love, although I got close to with Nova. Never had a real girlfriend. Just screwed and screwed and screwed.

But I'm over Nova for the most part and happy for both her and Quinton. Well, as long as they don't make out in front of me. That gets old really fast.

"So where are we going to go celebrate?" I ask, digging through my bag for a clean shirt. We stay in motel rooms when we're on the road, living out of suitcases. The motel rooms are usually pretty crappy, but anything's better than the run-down trailer homes and crack houses I've lived in over the years.

The motel we're staying at right now has got a nice view of junkyard across the street, but it's only a couple of miles from the house we're building so it makes it easy to walk there. Nova and Quinton share the adjoining room next door, which allows me to hear noises I'd rather not hear. Right now, he's wandered into my room and seated himself at the table near the window.

"Nova wanted to try that restaurant out on the north side of town." He's smoking a cigarette, the window cracked open so the smoke mostly goes outside.

It makes the need to feed my own nicotine habit rise and I take one out of my pack and light up, breathing in the sweet taste that feeds my craving. "A restaurant." I frown, picking up the ashtray on the nightstand. "Seems kind of boring."

Quinton sighs as he puts his cigarette out in the ashtray and gets to his feet. "Look, you know there's no way she's going to let us both go to a bar."

"Well, she technically can only tell one of us to do stuff." I make a whipping sound and motion my hand, pretending to crack a whip. It's all fun and games, although I kind of mean it. He is whipped. I remember the days when we'd just sit around and get high and do nothing. I sometimes miss it, miss the stillness, and the lack of responsibility to do anything. Day by day. That's what we did. But then again, we were kind of lucky to make it to the end of the day alive.

He rolls his eyes at me, but doesn't argue. "Whatever man. You know as well as I do that you'll come out with us."

I balance my cigarette on the ashtray so I can tug my shirt over my head. "Fine, what time are we leaving?" I ask, picking my cigarette back up.

He checks his watch and then nods at the door. "Let's get going now. We have to pick up Nova from the site and then we'll take a cab downtown."

"Fine, give me just a second." I put out my cigarette, go into the bathroom to put on some deodorant and cologne when my phone rings from my pocket. I check the screen and see it's my mother. I hate talking to her and I almost ignore it, but then realize that if I do, she'll excessively call me all night.

"What's up?" I answer, balancing the phone between my ear and shoulder why I spray on some cologne.

"Hey sweetie," she says sweetly and I can tell she's on her meds by the sound of euphoria in her voice. It's Ryder's birthday tomorrow and she always gets overly emotional during it and ends up having to take a few sedatives over the course of the week until her emotions pass. The first time I got high was actually from her stash. "I was just calling to see when you were going to be home."

I grab my wallet off the bathroom counter and tuck it in my back pocket. "I already told you, I can't make it out there right now, Mom." I fuck around with my blond hair, trying to get it out of my face, but it's gotten too long and keeps falling into my eyes, so I give up.

She gives a really long, drawn-out sigh. "Tristan, you have to. It's Ryder's birthday."

"It was my birthday a couple of weeks ago," I remind her. "And you didn't even call me."

"I'm sorry I forgot…but this is important. You need to be here."

"It's not that simple," I tell her, leaning against the wall, staring at the mirror across from me. I can see me so should she, right. *I do exist.* "I'm in North Carolina right now."

"North Carolina? Why are you way out there? It's so far from Wyoming." The longer she talks, the higher she sounds and the more pointless I realize this conversation is. "Look, I have to go, Mom. I'm headed out."

"With who?" She pauses. "You're going out with *him*, aren't you?"

I should just lie to her. It'd be easier if I did. But I hate lying and I hate that she wants to push me to hold grudges against Quinton. I've made my peace with it. Accidents are accidents. Shit happens. And holding on to it is tiring. "If you mean Quinton, then yeah." I head toward the door. "Look, we've been over this. You can stay mad at him if you want. Do what you have to do, but I'm choosing to let it go."

"Let your sister go," she gasps. "Tristan Morganson, how dare you. Don't you say that. Don't you dare."

I stop in front of the door and press my fingertips to the bridge of my nose. There's no point in this conversation. We've had the same one for years and it's becoming a broken record. "Look, Mom, I have to go. We're going out to celebrate me being disease free," I say, knowing she won't acknowledge it—anything related to my drug days she won't, because she's ashamed of me. I open the door. "Call me tomorrow if you feel like it."

"You're a terrible son." It's her last attempt to make me feel guilty, to lure me home.

"I know," I say, slipping on one of my boots. "And I'm sorry for that. Tell Dad I said hi."

"Tell him yourself," she snaps. "I'm not your messenger."

"Bye, Mom." I hang up the phone and stuff it into the back

pocket of my jeans before I put my other boot on and step outside. It's still hot and muggy, but that's June in North Carolina.

Quinton is outside smoking, sitting on the curb just in front of the door. I'm surprised to see Nova sitting beside him, since we were supposed to be picking her up. She's talking to Quinton, her blue eyes are all lit up, so she's excited about something. She's still wearing her work clothes, jeans and a black tank top, her brown hair braided to the side. Her face is sun-kissed and she looks gorgeous, but she's not mine and I shouldn't be thinking about her that way.

When she leans in and kisses Quinton, I almost back up and sneak into my room, pretend I'm sick, just so I won't have to see it, but mid-kiss she must sense I'm there because she opens her eyes and smiles at me.

"Hey you." Her smile brightens as she stands up and walks over to me. "Congrats, by the way. I've been meaning to tell you that all day."

Leave it to Nova to congratulate me on being disease free. "What, just congrats?" I joke. "What, no card?"

She lets out an exaggerated sigh, her lips quirking with amusement. "Sorry, but I couldn't find one for your exact situation. I think I'm going to call up the card companies and suggest that they need a hep C-free line." She grins.

"Oh, I'm sure that'll go over well," I say as Quinton joins us, handing me a cigarette as he lights up one himself. "I can just picture it now. A needle on the front and inside 'Congrats on not being a disgusting user anymore.'" Just talking about the needle makes my veins throb with need.

Nova's face instantly falls and Quinton shoots me a warning. "What's wrong?" Nova asks. "You should be happy, but you're not."

She's right. I'm not. I don't think I ever really have been. Half the time I'm not even sure why, but today I know. My mom's got me feeling guilty about Ryder and her birthday. I envied the high I could hear in my mom's voice, not just because it'll take all the emotional pain away but because it's easier to deal with being so alone when I'm out of it. But I'm good at faking being happy and I plaster a smile on my face. "Sorry. I just didn't sleep very well last night... I had a lot of stuff on my mind."

Nova leans in closer. "You want to talk about it?"

I shake my head, popping the cigarette into my mouth and then reaching into my pocket to get my lighter. "No, I'm good, but thanks." I inch away from her and light up as she leans back. "I am fucking hungry, though. So how about we go eat." I say it because it's what she wants to hear and it'll get her to leave me alone so I can sulk in my own head because what I really want to doing is snort lines. I know it's wrong. Know I'm fucked up for not being able to stop. But I've accepted that I might always be that way. An addict and I'm about to fuck up again, be the loser I am. But I tell myself I need it, that I can't live without it, because it makes it easier to do.

## Chapter 3

Nova has to get ready and Quinton goes back into the room with her. It's the perfect opportunity for me to take care of my craving. So I pretend to go back into my room, then I slip outside unnoticed and walk to the last door of the motel. There's a guy there who call himself D-Man. I ran into him once when I was wandering around outside. He was totally a tweaker: skinny, thinning hair, pale skin, bones protruding, teeth rotting, sores on his skin. It was looking into a mirror of the past and after chatting for a little while, I ended up doing a line with him, hence my slipup a few weeks ago. Quinton was the one who found out. Ex-tweakers have a radar for people who are spun out of their minds. He stayed with me until my system was clean, until the crashing was over, and he's been watching me like a hawk every since. He didn't tell Nova about it, which I'm grateful for. The last thing I want to do is see the disappointment in her eyes that I've seen many times before, including when I kissed her. That one stung.

I rap on the door and he opens up, his eyes glossed over with that look I crave. I need to make it quick before I get busted, so I say I need to buy a hit, or two, or three, or four.

"Sure man," he says, his voice in that same euphoric state as my mother's. He goes back into the room and I wait outside because I can see the syringe and spoon on his nightstand and I know if I step over the threshold I'll want to do that, but I can't. Not without being busted the moment I pass out. Plus that's the cause behind why we're going out to celebrate that I'm disease free today. Still, I crave it and I think I pretty much keep my eyes on it the entire time until D-Man comes back with a small bag with a pinch of white crystals in it. I give him the money, and then tuck it into my pocket, hurrying back toward my room so I'll have time to do it before we go out.

But my plan goes to shit because Quinton's waiting outside when I get there, smoking, and when he sees me coming, he gets this weird look on his face like his tweaker radar is on.

"Where've you been?" he asks, ashing his cigarette as he searches my eyes, probably for enlarged pupils and lack of blinking.

I miss a beat, but recover. "I went to see if they have any gum in the vending machines," I say, pointing over my shoulder. "If we're going to a restaurant, I'm not going to be able to smoke when I want to and I'm going to need something to keep me from wanting to grind the shit out of my teeth all night."

He's not buying it, but doesn't press. "Nova will be out in just a second," he says and plops down on the curb, stretching out his legs. He doesn't ask me to sit down and I could easily slip back into my room and do my line. It'd make tonight a hell of a lot easier to bear. But I know if I do, he's going to sense something else is up, and honestly, I don't want him to know that I'm still that person who runs to drugs every time there's a bump in the road. Or maybe I'm just deciding what road I want to go down.

# Chapter 4

Quinton and I sit on the curb while we wait for Nova to come out. We smoke and stare as the blue sky shifts to gray. It's fairly quiet and we only talk every few minutes. It reminds me of when we were both doing drugs and we just sit and let time waste away. It makes it difficult not to pull out the bag and say "Let's take a hit," and it makes the bag feel like it's burning a hole in my pocket. *I'm going to have to find a way to get alone so I can do it.*

About fifteen minutes later, Nova walks out of their room wearing shorts and a clean tank top, her hair down and running down her back in waves. "Okay, so Avery should be here any second."

"Who the hell is Avery?" I ask as Quinton says, "Sounds good."

Nova shuts the door, slinging her purse over her shoulder. "Oh, she's the girl whose house we're building. She actually stopped by today and we got talking and I said how we were going out to celebrate. She mentioned she knew some good places with good music and offered to take us out as a thank-you." She plops down on the curb between Quinton and me. "She's really nice. I think you'll like her."

I rake my fingers through my hair. Great. One more person I'm going to have to escape tonight. "What exactly did you say we're celebrating?"

"Life," Nova says simply. I press back a smile. Only her.

A moment later a horn beeps and Nova glances around the parking lot and then waves at this old red Jeep with the top off parked just a ways off. "There she is." She gets up and heads over and Quinton and I follow her.

"You okay with this?" Quinton asks quietly cross the parking lot.

"With what?" I ask, patting my pocket to make sure I have my cigarettes and lighter on me.

"With going out with a stranger on your night?"

"My night?" I say in a sarcastic tone. "You make it sound like I'm a sixteen-year-old girl going to prom."

He snorts a laugh. "You know what I mean."

I shrug. "Yeah, I'm fine with whoever goes. It's all the same."

He nods and then slows down as we reach the Jeep. He opens the door to get in and the girl…Avery or whatever says hi to him as he flips the seat back and climbs in. I follow, letting Nova take the front. As I'm getting situated in the backseat, I get a good look at this Avery girl. When Nova said that there was a girl coming with us and that it was the one we were building the house for, I expected someone older. Avery has long brown hair with a streak of purple going down it, hazel eyes surrounded by black eyeliner, and full lips with a piercing just above the top one. She's got to be around twenty, give or take a few years, which has me confused why we're building her a house. She looks like she should be in college. Usually when we build houses, they're for families.

"I'm Avery," she says as she turns in her seat and extends her hand to me. I notice she has a cross tattooed on her forearm with the word *Survivor* below it. I wonder what she's survived.

"Tristan," I say, taking her hand and shaking it. There's this weird moment between the two of us where I sense that she's checking me out just as much as I'm checking her out. She's not bad on the eyes at all. Totally fuckable. She looks like she's been through some stuff, rough around the edges, eyes that carry secrets. I wonder what those secrets are—I wonder if they're as fucked up as mine.

"Nice to meet you, Tristan," she says, giving me a once-over, in this slow, lasting way.

She takes one last look then turns to Quinton, smiling, but it doesn't quite reach her eyes. "And good to see you again, Quinton."

"Likewise," Quinton says as Nova hops into the front seat and closes the door. "So where are you taking us?"

Avery grabs the shifter as she turns on the headlights. "I was thinking about going to the The Vibe. They've got some really good food and music and it's not as rowdy as some of the other shit around here." She drives onto the road, the wind sweeping through the roofless vehicle. "You guys are all twenty-one, right?" She specifically glances at me from over her shoulder and I almost laugh. That's a first. Usually people think I'm older.

"I'm twenty-three," I tell her, then just because, I decided to throw it back at her. "You don't look old enough, though."

"Twenty-two." She winks. "But I'll take that as a compliment."

"I meant it as a compliment." And now I'm flirting.

Quinton glances at me, arching a brow, like *Really, you're going to go there?* Avery seems to enjoy it, still smiling as she turns around in her seat.

"What?" I ask him, playing dumb.

"Nothing." He shakes his head, then leans toward me. "Be careful, man. Remember, she's the person we're building a house for and it's not going to go over well if you hook up with her and bail out the next morning."

I glance up front to see if Nova and Avery are paying attention, but they're chatting about bands. Nova plays the drums and Avery plays the guitar and they both seem excited about this.

"Who said I'm planning on hooking up and bailing on her?" I ask quietly.

"You have that look in your eyes."

"What look?"

He gives me an accusing look. "The one you get right before you hook up and then leave the girl two seconds later. I know the drill man. I used to do it too, remember."

"Hey, maybe I'm planning on hooking up with her and sticking around for a while," I say.

"In the four years we've been around each other," he says. "I've never seen you ever once stick around."

I want to tell him that's not true. That I stuck around for Nova, even when we didn't hook up. I almost do too, mainly so he'll get pissed and I can go get high without worrying about him keeping an eye on me. But Nova and Avery are in the car and I don't know Avery and Nova's seen enough of the ugly in me for a while. So I keep my lips shut and I kind of zone out for the rest of the drive, thinking about Ryder. I feel bad for not going home, but not because of my mother. Ryder was a good sister. Things were easier when she was there. When I was younger, she saw me when I was invisible to everyone else in my family. *I should have gone home, if nothing else, for her.*

Guilt creeps up inside me and I want nothing more than to quiet it the one way I know how. I put my hand into my pocket and feel the plastic in the palm of my hand. God, what I'd give to pull it out now.

The sky gets darker as we merge into the heart of the small town, the buildings lining the sides of the roads lighting up the night with their signs and flashing lights. I start flicking my lighter restlessly, needing to light up, but I'm not about to do it somebody else's car. So I wait until we're parked, then I hop out and quickly light up, feeling my heart and thoughts still. Quinton lights up too, and then Avery surprises me when she asks to borrow my lighter so she can light up as well.

"Wow, I feel like I'm about to get cancer," Nova jokes as we walk toward the front door with a cloud of smoke around us.

"Oh, do you want me to put is out?" Avery asks, bending down like she's going to put it out on the ground. She's got a nice body, leggy, a tight ass. She's wearing a tight black dress with boots, the back of her dress low and revealing a tattoo of a tree, half dead, half flourishing. The flourishing half has leaves blowing away from it and below it the words: *Carry me away, to where I can breathe, to where my soul can thrive again, to where I can be free to where I can live again.* There's more too it than that, but it goes below the dress. I'm curious what the rest of it says. I have my own tattoos with their own meanings and that kind of a tattoo has to have a meaning. Maybe it's her life story. It makes me wonder if I can get under the dress to see if she was able to live again and why she thought she was dying.

"So do you have any of your own?"

I jerk from my thoughts and realize that Avery is standing to the side of me and Nova and Quinton have migrated to the front. "Any of my own what?" I ask distracted by how intense Avery's eyes are up close—this girl has definitely been through some stuff.

She reaches around and touches her back. "Tats." Her hand falls to her side. "I saw you staring at mine."

"Oh." I take a drag from my cigarette, thinking of what Quinton said about staying away from her and how I want to do the opposite at the moment. "A few here and there."

Her eyes scroll over my body and she smiles, but it's a ghost smile, masking this tremendous amount of pain her eyes carry. "Leaving it up to my imagination, huh?"

I'm not sure if she's just being friendly or flirting, but I'm going with the latter because it gives me a good excuse for what I do next. "One on my ribs. One on my arm. The third one's a secret." I wink at her. "Maybe I'll show it to you later."

Her expression never wavers, making it hard to unravel her. And flirt. She ashes her cigarette before taking a drag off it. "Any of them mean anything?"

"They all do." I arch a brow at her. "Yours?"

She nods, biting her lip. "All five of them."

I want to ask her about the one on her back, but we're approaching the line in front of the entrance to the place we're going to and the crowd's voices silence me.

"You guys wait here," Avery says, walking back toward the front of the line with a finger held up. "I'll be right back."

As soon as she's out of sight, Nova says, "Are you guys going to be okay with this place?"

Quinton glances at the door then back at her. "As much as I love you, you need to relax. We've been to clubs before, even after we got clean."

I discreetly catch Quinton glancing at me, which means he's worried about me, but isn't going to say anything to Nova because it'll only make her worry more.

"I should have told her no places with alcohol," Nova mutters, frowning at the ground.

"Every place has alcohol," I tell her, then playfully nudge her shoulder. "Would you relax? We'll be fine." I lift up my hand as if making a vow. "And I won't drink. I promise." *I'll just do the line in my pocket.*

She still seems concerned, but gets distracted when Avery comes skipping back with a half-smoked cigarette in her mouth and three pink bands in her hand and one around her wrist. "Here. Put these on." She hands us each a band, looking very proud of herself. "And follow me."

"What about the line?" Nova asks as she puts the band on her wrist.

Avery pulls her cigarette out of her mouth. "I have connections." She turns around to head to the front, giving me another once-over, looking like she's trying to be nonchalant about the fact that she's checking me out, but falters a little. It makes it really hard not to just grab her and kiss her. I'm not that kind of guy, though. I'm honestly not even sure when the last time I just made out with a girl was. I've fucked a lot of girls, ones I didn't know, ones that were high—I was high. I'm not even sure if I know how to just kiss.

We follow Avery to the front of the line and the bouncer lets us right through, giving Avery a kiss on the cheek as she walk by and muttering something about being sorry to hear about Conner. The name makes her expression falter, but she quickly recovers and plaster a fake smile on her face. Boy, she's fucking good. It always takes me a beat or two to fake it. She must have a lot of practice. Why, though?

"Thanks," she says to the bouncer, then opens the door and we follow her inside the club.

The lighting is low, like it is in most clubs. The music loud and bass throbbing. The air smells like smoke, sweat, and booze. There's a dance floor that gives everyone an excuse to rub up against each other until they all become so horny they have to pair off and go back for a one-night stand. I know the scene. Lived it for a long, long time, and it makes me want to live it again. Maybe Nova's right. We probably should have avoided places like this tonight.

We find a table in the back corner where it's less noisy. Nova and Quinton sit down and Nova picks up a menu. I'm glancing around, looking for the bathroom, not because I have to piss, but because I need to do this line before it drives me insane.

"You want to come with me to get drinks?" Avery asks me. She has this accusing look on her face and I swear she knows exactly what I was just thinking. But how could she? No one possibly could.

"Sure," I tell her, one single word that's really fucking hard to get out.

"You guys want anything?" Avery asks Nova and Quinton.

"A water's fine," Quinton says, but I can tell it's a little difficult for him to say it when we're here in a room full of booze.

"A diet Coke," Nova says, opening up the menu. Her gaze flicks to me for a moment and I can tell she's wondering what I'm going to come back with.

"Relax," I say to her, just so she'll stop. "I'll be a good boy. I promise."

That gets her to smile.

I follow Avery to the bar area where she leans over the counter, trying to flag down the bartender. Her dress rides up and I get a glimpse of this unique flower symbol-type tattoo on the back of her thigh. That makes three I've seen. Only two more to go.

"Hey Benny, would you hurry your ass up," Avery calls out playfully to the bartender, who glances over at her and grins.

"Keep your panties on," he says as he pours some shots. God, it's been a while since I've had a shot. "I'll be over in a second."

Avery laughs and then settles on a barstool, her eyes landing on me. "So are you going to sit down or just stand there?"

She's got me thrown off a little. Very blunt. Very forward, or at least that's how it seems. But like I said, there's this look in her eyes like she's trying to keep a lot of secrets buried.

I drop down on the stool and rest my arms on the countertop. "You come here a lot? You seem to know a lot of people around here."

"Well, I should," she says with a twinkle in her eyes. "Since I work here every afternoon from noon to five."

I want to ask her why she's in desperate need for a house, but I don't want to make her uncomfortable, so I opt for option number two. "So what's the tattoo on the back of your leg mean?"

She smiles at me again in this dark, mysterious sort of way. "You noticed that one, huh?"

I nod. "Yeah, while you were flagging the bartender down."

She rolls her tongue in her mouth like she's trying not to laugh. "When you were checking out my ass?"

I could deny it, but I don't want to. "Hey, it's a nice ass. It's hard not to look at it."

That gets her to laugh. "I knew it," she says, shaking her head with a grin as she looks ahead at the mirror in front of us.

I lean forward to catch her gaze. "Knew what?"

She laughs a little more, amused with whatever she's thinking. "That you were one of *those* guys."

"Those guys?" I'm curious what she means.

She doesn't answer right away or look at me. The song switches from this poppy, silly one to "All the Same" by Sick Puppies and I'm grateful because I hate club music.

Finally she looks me, slowly scanning me over from head to toe. "Blond hair, pretty blue eyes, a charming smile. You're one of those guys who knows he's hot and knows just the right thing to make a girl swoon or whatever."

"Swoon?" I question, trying not to laugh. "Really?"

She shrugs. "Hey, I'm just saying it how it is. I totally hate the word." She points a finger at me, her smile still there. "And I never do it. Ever."

"So you're saying that my blond hair, pretty blue eyes," I wink at her, "and hotness aren't affecting you at all."

She shakes her head, eyes locked on me. "I don't do pretty boys."

"Who said I was a pretty boy? What if I'm a bad boy underneath it all?"

"I don't do bad boys either."

I lean in, catching her scent. It's nice, some sort of perfume mixed with vanilla. "Then what do you do?"

She shakes her head, biting her lip again. "Nothing. Work. Go to school. Go home. That's all."

"So no guys?"

"Nope, no guys." She seems pretty adamant about it.

I'm not sure what to do with this information. On the one hand it means she doesn't have a boyfriend, but on the other hand it also means she doesn't want one or any guy for that matter. Maybe she likes girls.

"I'm not a lesbian," she says as if she can read my thoughts for the second time tonight. "I'm just not interested in dating, having a relationship, or fucking around for many, many different reasons." All her humor vanishes and all I can see is pain. It's almost overwhelming to look at and I want to look away but I can't seem to bring myself to do so. So we end up just staring at each other, unable to look away, yet unable to find anything to say.

Thankfully, the bartender comes over and interrupts us. "So

what are you doing here tonight on your night off?" he asks, leaning over the counter toward Avery.

Avery nonchalantly shrugs, tearing her gaze off me and fixes it on him. "I was bored. Thought I'd get out of the house for a while."

"Good. You need to," he says and I catch him glancing down the top of her dress. In the middle of it, he notices me noticing his not so discreet checking out. "Who are you?" he asks Avery, and I can tell right away that he must have a thing for her or something by the coldness in his tone.

"This is Tristan," Avery tells him. "He's one of the people helping build my house."

"Oh." He relaxes and gives me a chin nod. "It's nice to meet you, man."

"Likewise," I say, deciding maybe it's time to make that trip to the bathroom so I can get on with my night plans.

"So what do you guys want to drink?" he asks. "First round on the house, for giving this beautiful and very deserving girl over here a roof over her head."

"I'll just have a Coke," I tell him, wishing I could say *with a bit of Jack Daniel's in it.*

"All right." He looks at Avery. "And I'm guessing just the usual diet Coke for you."

"Two actually. And one water." She points over her shoulder at where Quinton and Nova are sitting with a menu opened up in front of them, but their focused on each other, not picking something out to eat. "I'm here with a few more people."

"All right. Be back in a sec." He leaves to get our drinks.

"So you don't drink either, huh?" Avery asks me, fixing her attention back on me.

I shake my head. "Not really."

"And neither does Nova and Quinton, I take it."

"Yeah, are you getting excited? You get to spend the night with a bunch of boring, sober people," I joke with a forced smile.

"I'm glad," she says. "It makes it easier to keep my own sobriety."

That shocks me a little. "For how long?"

She touches her collarbone, where there's another tattoo. "Two years, three months, and fifteen days," she tells me as I read the black ink on her smooth, flawless skin. *Never forget the strength it took to free yourself.* "How long has it been for you?"

"I'm not a recovering alcoholic," I say, my eyes flicking back to hers.

"Then what are you?" she asks with her head angled to the side, strands of her hair framing her face; strands I want to brush back and tuck behind her ear, but I won't.

I'm not sure whether to tell her the truth. It's hard to say how she'll react. People tend to get a little scared when you mention drugs, especially things like meth and heroin. I open my mouth, fully intending just to tell her weed, but the truth comes out.

"I was into heroin and meth pretty hardcore for a while," I say and I swear to God the bag of meth in my pocket jumps out and says: *And he's about to do it again.*

I expect her to ask how long I've been clean, but she says, "That's good. That you got cleaned up from that I mean." She seems really nervous and reaches for a napkin and starts shredding it to pieces. "I've heard that stuff can really ruin your life." The way she says it has me wondering if she's speaking from experience. Not personally, but maybe someone close to her.

"That tattoo on your neck." Before I can stop myself, I graze my finger across it. I quickly pull my hand away, playing it off as cool, when really I want to leave my fingers there, feel the softness of her skin just a little bit longer. "You got that when you got clean?"

She tries to appear calm, but I detect a hint of a shiver, perhaps from my touch. She peels off another piece of the napkin. "Once I hit the one-year marker." She traces her finger over the tattoo and this time I notice there's a scar above it, right across her throat. It's faint but still there, across her skin. Her finger trembles as she touches the scar, then drops her hand to the countertop. "So what's it like building a house?"

It's clear she wants a subject change so I give it to her. "Honestly?" I ask and she nods. "Hot and boring."

She laughs, finally shoving the napkin to the side and looking at me again and not in a way that she has to look at me because we're sitting here, chatting. She's looking at me like she wants to look at me, like she's fully noticing me now, like she's enjoying sitting here beside me. "So why are you doing it then?"

I nod toward Nova and Quinton without taking my eyes off her. "Those two are into it and they asked me to come with them." I pause. "They keep me out of trouble."

She nods. "Gotcha. So then they're kind of like you're sponsors or something."

"Yeah, something like that," I say, not wanting to get into the details of our complicated triangle.

She's about to say something else when suddenly someone says something really loud and her attention snaps to the side of us. I sense her tense up, her hands balling into fists, her jaw setting tight. I turn to find what's got her so scared and see a guy striding toward us through the crowd with his eyes focused solely on her as he pushes people out of his path. He looks rough around the edges; short hair, goatee, arms covered in tattoos that go up to his shoulders and his neck.

"Fuck," she utters under her breath. "I can't handle this shit tonight."

I'm about to ask her what when the guy reaches us. "You didn't call me back," he says to Avery.

"That's because I had nothing to say." Avery reaches for her napkin and starts ripping it to pieces.

He moves around to the back of her and her whole body goes rigid. "We need to fucking talk, Avery. You can't just keep ignoring me."

"Of course I can," she says, staring ahead instead of at him. "Besides, you're not even supposed to be talking to me at all. Court's orders."

Shit. This is the last thing I want to get in the middle of. I'm about to get up and walk away, go to the bathroom and do my thing, when the guys says, "Who the fuck is this?"

I've had my ass kicked many times. I'm an ex-junkie who used to deal and steal and mess with the wrong people. In fact, I almost got killed over it once. That alone should have me getting up and leaving, because this guy seems like the kind who would start swinging with no real cause except for he thinks I'm doing something to him. But Avery looks at me with this plea in her eyes that says *Please don't leave me.*

"He's just a friend, Conner," she says tightly. "So don't do anything stupid."

Conner. The guy the bouncer was talking about.

Conner stares me down, trying to intimidate me and I stare right back, refusing to look away, knowing what it'll mean if I do. Finally, he's the one who gives up and looks back at Avery.

"Can I talk to you in private?" he asks, leaning in toward her.

"No," Avery says, attempting to sound firm, but there's fear in her voice. Why is this girl afraid of him? I wonder if it has to do with the scar on her neck.

"It's about Mason," Conner says.

"Don't you dare say his name," she snaps, shoving him back. "You don't even deserve to say it."

Rage flares in Conner's eyes and suddenly he has Avery by the arm and is dragging her through the crowd toward the back of the building. Part of me is screaming at myself to stay out of it but the other part of me wants to run after them.

I hesitate, deciding what I'm going to do. "Fuck," I say and then get up from the stool, pushing after them, wondering just how big of a mess I'm running after. And if I can handle it.

# Chapter 5

When I reach them, Avery is jerking her arm, trying to get it out of his hold as he slams his hand against the back door and steps outside. I follow a few moments later and by the time I get out there, he's got her trapped against the wall by the Dumpster and is already yelling at her. I can tell he's definitely done something to hurt her in the past, by the way she flinches every time he raises his voice. I'm going back and forth with whether to go back inside or step in. Do I want to get into this mess? Can I handle this mess?

"You made it sound worse than it was," he shouts, getting in her face, veins bulging in his neck. "This is bullshit."

She hugs her arms around herself. "All I did was tell the truth, you fucking asshole," she yells back, but her voice cracks.

"You are such a fucking liar," he says, slamming his hand against the Dumpster and causing her to wince. "A fucking alcoholic just like your mother."

"I'm nothing like my mother," she shouts back, getting brave enough to get in his face. "And I'm sober now. And being a drunk is a hell of a lot better than what you are."

I see him raise his hand and my uncertainty whether to get into this mess vanishes in a heartbeat. I stride forward and shove him back, knowing this is all about to blow up in my face, especially when he ends up bashing his head into the Dumpster.

"Shit," Avery says, staring in horror at Connor as he works to regain his footing. She pushes me back toward the door without taking her eyes off him. "Tristan, go back inside."

I gape at her. "You're seriously trying to protect me right now."

She gives me another push, this time looking at me, and all I can see is fear in her eyes. "Trust me. It's for your own good."

I'm shaking my head, confused as hell, because this guy was just about to beat the crap out of her and she's trying to protect me instead of herself, when Conner gets to his feet.

"You're fucking dead, pretty boy," he says, reaching for his pocket, with this annoying smirk on his face.

What is with all the pretty boy comments tonight?

"Avery, let's go inside," I say, taking Avery buy the arm and guiding her behind me. I can sense something bad is about to happen. Whatever he's about to pull out of his pocket is not going to be a cigarette—that's for sure. It's a knife and not a small pocketknife, but a larger, hunting-type knife.

I've had a few guns pulled out on me before, knives, brass knuckles; it's nothing new. Yet it is. Because I'm sober. When I was high, it was easier to ignore the bigger picture. But I can fully see it now—how easily I could die if this guy wanted to kill me.

I instantly step in front of Avery and spread my hands out to the side, protecting her. "Go inside," I call over my shoulder.

"Just friends, huh?" Conner shakes his head, aggravated, as he moves toward us with the knife out in front of him. "I knew that shit couldn't be true. You're too much of a slut to have a friend that's a guy."

I hear Avery dialing someone on her cell phone from behind me. The cops I hope.

Seconds later, Conner takes a swing at me and I double back, but he ends up clipping my side. I stagger over my feet as the tip of the knife splits my shirt and grazes the skin. I quickly recover and throw a punch of my own, my fist connecting with his jaw. His eyes redden with anger and I'm not sure if hitting him was a good idea or not.

He lets out this growl and then dives at me with no control over his movements at all, like he would easily kill me and not care, but I jump to the side and he ends up ramming into the building wall behind us. He curses, then turns around, wiping some blood off his split lip. *Dead*, he mouths.

Avery shouts something and I hear sirens seconds later. Thank fucking God. Conner glances down at the end of the alley and then with no hesitation, he takes off running in the other direction, hopping over the fence at the end. I start to chase him down, when Avery yells, "No, don't." Her hand touches my arm. "Let him go."

I turn around. "Let him go? He just tried to kill me."

"If you chase him down, then he might finish the job," she says in a serious voice, her eyes wild with fear, and I can feel her pulse racing in her fingertips.

I settle my breathing before I speak again. "Are you okay?"

She gapes at me. "I'm fine. But what about you?" She lifts up my shirt without even asking first. She examines the cut on my side, her fingers tracing gently around it, but I barely feel a thing, too busy watching her watching me. "It doesn't look too deep." Her voice quivers as she pulls down my shirt down. "But you might want to get it checked out, just in case."

"It's fine. I've had worse," I tell her. The fear and pain in her eyes tell me so has she. We stand there for a moment, just staring at each other, breathing in and out. I have no idea what the hell is going on, not just between her and me, but with her and that Conner guy. I'm about to ask her, when the cops show up.

We end up answering a few questions and filing a report. Nova and Quinton come out when I text them. I pick up bits and pieces of the conversation between Avery and the cops and put together enough that Conner is her ex-husband and that he just got out of jail for something. I want to ask her a ton of questions and I'm planning on doing so, but I never get the chance. After the police leave, we all get into the Jeep and she drives us back to the motel. Nova asks her a few questions, but Avery is vague and Nova being Nova senses that Avery doesn't want to talk about it and instantly drops the questioning. I think about staying in the car when we pull up to the motel. I just want to know... well, I'm not sure what I want to know. If she's okay? If she's going to be okay? But Quinton ushers me out, despite me giving him a dirty look.

I'm heading back to my motel room when I hear Avery say, "Hey, Tristan, can I talk to you for a minute?"

"Yeah," I call out, hoping I'll get an explanation. I tell Nova and Quinton that I'll meet them inside. Then I turn around and jog back to the Jeep. Avery has the window rolled down and she's not looking at me, but just over my shoulder, in Nova and Quinton's direction.

"What's up?" I ask as I reach the Jeep.

She holds up a finger. "Just a second." She waits until Nova and Quinton disappear into the room, then her eyes land on me. She doesn't say anything right away, instead reaching down toward her boot and taking something out of it.

My face instantly falls when I see what it is. "Where did you get that?" I ask in a tight voice.

She holds the bag of crystal in her hand and it takes a lot of energy not to rip it from her. "It fell out of your pocket when you were fighting Conner," she says, staring at it. "I picked it up and tucked it into my boot when the police came. I was going to just dump it down the toilet when I got home, but then I…" She trails off, looking at me.

"But you wanted to see why I had it," I finish for her.

She nods. "I thought you said you were clean."

I try to act cool about it, but her disappointed gaze makes me feel guilty for some reason. Obviously this girl's been through shit and she managed to get sober. I can't get my dumb ass clean for more than a couple of weeks at a time. "I did, but I never said for how long."

"How long?" she asks, her eyes searching mine.

"Three weeks," I say, holding her gaze.

She considers what I said without looking away from me. "What do you want me to do with it?"

"You're seriously giving me choice?" *Is this girl for real?*

"It doesn't really matter if I get rid of it," she says. "If you don't want me to, then you'll just go get some more."

Those are the words of someone who understands being an addict. It makes me hate her and really fucking like her at the same time. "What if I said I wanted it back?" I ask. "Would you give it to me?"

She thinks about it and nods with reluctance. "If that's what you wanted."

I consider what I want. *Her*, my mind screams. It makes me want to ask her to come back to my room, but I decided to be a nice guy for one night—do something good for a change, even though it just about kills me just thinking about it. But she did just almost get her ass kicked by her ex-husband.

"You can dump it down the toilet when you get home," I say,

even though it's painful to say it. My pulse accelerates from the words and my palms dampen. It feels like I'm being strangled.

She blows out a breath, relaxing. "If that's what you want," she says with a hint of amusement and it makes me smile just a little. She puts the bag back in her boot and reaches for the shifter, about to drive away. I start to leave when she says, "Oh and Tristan."

I pause and turn to face her. "Yeah."

She hesitates, considering something for a moment, then ultimately leans out her window and presses her lips to mine. It's a quick kiss. No tongue, but there's a lot of emotion behind it. I feel my heart rate quicken for a split second. Then she's pulling away. "Thanks," she says, biting her lip. "For stepping in. Not a lot of people would have done that." She doesn't saying anything else and doesn't give me time to respond, driving away into the night, leaving me with a thousand questions running through my head.

And the biggest need to kiss her again.

# Chapter 6

I'm anxious the next day to get some information about Avery. While we're walking to the site on the side of the road, I ask Nova if she'll give me Avery's number, even though I'm not sure if I should call her.

"What happened last night?" Nova asks as she kicks rocks up on the side of the road with her feet. "Seriously, Tristan. Avery seemed really upset and you had that cut on your side..." She glances down at my ribs.

"I already told you what I know," I say with my hands stuffed inside my pockets of my jeans. "Her ex-husband showed up and tried to beat her up, so I helped her out."

"Well, it was very brave of you," Nova says, pulling her sunglasses over her head and taking a sip of her coffee. "And kind of stupid."

"I'm going to second that," Quinton says, reaching for his cigarettes in his pocket. "I think we've gotten in enough fights to last us a lifetime."

"Yeah, I know. But I doubt that will be my last," I say, tossing him his lighter that I borrowed earlier.

Quinton shakes his head again as he lights up. He doesn't say anything more, putting the lighter in his pocket and puffing on his cigarette.

"Well, I don't have her number," Nova says with an apologetic look. "But I'm sure she'll be there today, since the house will be finished up. I think I even heard her say something about picking up the keys. She seemed really excited about it."

I nod, unsure if it's a good thing or a bad one that I'm eager to see her again. I keep telling myself that it's because I want answer to what the hell last night was about—nothing more. But there's a voice in the back of my head, telling me I'm wrong. That it had to do with the kiss, wanting to see all of her tattoos, and the fact that I dreamt about her last night, over and over again.

"Do you know why she needs the house?" I wonder, trying to seem like I'm just asking it to make conversation.

Nova shakes her head. "She didn't mention it and I didn't want to ask her, just in case it was something painful."

I nod and then make the rest of the walk in silence. I try my best to get through the day without thinking about Avery too much, helping out with the finishing touches on the house. It's probably the hardest I've worked in a long time and when I'm done, I'm tired and ready to head back to the motel to sleep. But instead I help clean up, hoping Avery will come by before we leave. *Just to get some answers*, I keep telling myself.

But eventually, all the tools are packed up and Avery still hasn't shown up. The sun is descending below the hills and there's nothing left to do but leave. I'm sitting on the cooler in front of the house, staring at the sunset when Nova walks up to me.

"She left town for a while," Nova says, taking a seat beside me on the cooler.

"Who?" I play dumb, eyes fixed on the light slipping away behind the hills.

"The person you've been pretending not to look for all day." She nudges her shoulder into mine. "This woman showed up and was talking to someone about Avery having to leave town for a little and that she was supposed to pick up the house keys for her." She pauses. "I can go ask the woman for Avery's number if you want."

I shake my head, brushing my hair out of my eyes. "Nah, that's okay."

"Are you sure?" Nova asks. "It's not a big deal."

I pause, trying to sift through all my thoughts. What is the real reason I want to talk to Avery so much? Is it because I want answers or is there more to it than that? I mean, I barely know her. Hell, I don't even know her last name. Yet I'm extremely curious about her, want to get to know her. Attracted to her. But seriously, what would be the point? We'd chat for like five minutes and then tomorrow I'd be gone. That would be the end of it. Besides, it's probably for the better. I'm not the kind of person she needs in her life, I'm sure. Some ex-junkie who slips up pretty much every other week. I can't even keep my own shit together and the girl seems like she has a lot of her own shit to deal with. Still, it's hard to just walk away.

"Yeah, I'm sure," I say to Nova, but for some reason, it feels like I'm making the biggest mistake of my life.

Nova looks sad, but nods and gets to her feet. "How about I go find Quinton and then we can take off?" She stretches her arms above her head. "I'm really tired."

I get to my own feet. "Sounds good. I got to run inside and grab something and then I'll meet you guys by the truck."

We part ways and I go into the house, not to get anything like I said, but to do something I'm not sure I should be doing. I don't even know what compels me to do it. I've had people come and go through my life, over and over again. Hardly any of them I can remember. Some are just ghost memories. And I've completely forgotten most. I'm not sure that I'll ever forget Avery completely. I'm not sure whether it's because of the crazy stuff that happened or because for a moment it seemed like we shared a moment.

So I go into the kitchen and find a pen someone left on one of the counters, probably used for measuring. Then I open one of the lower cupboards below the kitchen sink and crouch down in front of it. I know I could get into deep shit for doing this if anyone found out, but I've never been one to fear getting into trouble.

I lean into the cupboard and press the pen to the side of it, pausing before I write.

*Avery,*

*I'm not sure if you're okay, but I hope so. I know this is probably weird, some guy you met for like two seconds writing on your kitchen cupboard, but I just wanted to say that I hope you find the place where you can breathe, to where your soul can thrive again, to where you can be free, to where you can live again....I never really did see the rest of the tattoo so I'm not sure. Maybe you already have. I hope so.*

*It was nice meeting you. Hopefully one day our paths will cross again.*

*Tristan.*
*aka the pretty boy*

Love Tristan? Visit JessicaSorensen.com for updates on her latest releases.

Don't miss the beginning of Lila & Ethan's story.

See the next page for a preview of

## The Secret of Ella and Micha.

# Chapter 1

*8 months later…*

## Ella

I despise mirrors. Not because I hate my reflection or that I suffer from Eisoptrophobia. Mirrors see straight through my façade. They know who I used to be; a loud spoken, reckless girl, who showed what she felt to the world. There were no secrets with me.

But now secrets define me.

If a reflection revealed what was on the outside, I'd be okay. My long auburn hair goes well with my pale complexion. My legs are extensively long and with heels, I'm taller than most of the guys I know. But I'm comfortable with it. It's what's buried deep inside that frightens me because it's broken, like a shattered mirror.

I tape one of my old sketches over the mirror on the dorm wall. It's almost completely concealed by drawings and obscures all of my reflection except for my green eyes, which are frosted with infinite pain and secrets.

I pull my hair into a messy bun and place my charcoaled pencils into a box on my bed, packing them with my other art supplies.

Lila skips into the room with a cheery smile on her face and a drink in her hand. "Oh my God! Oh my God! I'm so glad it's over."

I pick up a roll of packing tape off the dresser. "Oh my God! Oh my god!" I joke. "What are you drinking?"

She tips the cup at me and winks. "Juice, silly. I'm just really excited to be getting a break. Even if it does mean I have to go home." She tucks strands of her hair behind her ear and tosses a makeup bag into her purse. "Have you seen my perfume?"

I point at the boxes on her bed. "I think you packed them in one of those. Not sure which one, though, since you didn't label them."

She pulls a face at me. "Not all of us can be neat freaks. Honestly, Ella, sometimes I think you have OCD."

I write "Art Supplies" neatly on the box and click the cap back on the sharpie. "I think you might be on to me," I joke.

"Dang it." She smells herself. "I really need it. All this heat is making me sweat." She rips some photos off her dresser mirror and throws them into an open box. "I swear it's like a hundred and ten outside."

"I think it's actually hotter than that." I set my school work in the trash, all marked with A's. Back in High School, I used to be a C student. I hadn't really planned on going to college, but life changes—people change.

Lila narrows her blue eyes at my mirror. "You do know that we're not going to have the same dorm when we come back in the fall, so unless you take all your artwork off, it's just going to be thrown out by the next person."

They're just a bunch of doodles; sketches of haunting eyes, black roses entwined by a bed of thorns, my name woven in an intricate pattern. None of them matter except one: a sketch of an old friend, playing his guitar. I peel that one off, careful not to tear the corners.

"I'll leave them for the next person," I say and add a smile. "They'll have a predecorated room."

"I'm sure the next person will actually want to look in the mirror." She folds up a pink shirt. "Although, I don't know why you want to cover up the mirror. You're not ugly, El."

"It's not about that." I stare at the drawing that captures the intensity in Micha's eyes.

Lila snatches the drawing from my hands, crinkling the edges a little. "One day you're going to have to tell me who this gorgeous guy is."

"He's just some guy I used to know." I steal the drawing back. "But we don't talk anymore."

"What's his name?" She stacks a box next to the door.

I place the drawing into the box and seal it with a strip of tape. "Why?"

She shrugs. "Just wondering."

"His name is Micha." It's the first time I've said his name aloud, since I left home. It hurts, like a rock lodged in my throat. "Micha Scott."

She glances over my shoulder as she piles the rest of her clothes into a box. "There's a lot of passion in that drawing. I just don't see him as being some guy. Is he like an old boyfriend or something?"

I drop my duffel bag, packed with my clothes, next to the door. "No, we never dated."

She eyes me over with doubt. "But you came close to dating? Right?"

"No. I told you we were just friends." But only because I wouldn't let us be anything more. Micha saw too much of me and it scared me too much to let him in all the way.

She twists her strawberry blonde hair into a ponytail and fans her face. "Micha is an interesting name. I think a name really says a lot about a person." She taps her manicured finger on her chin, thoughtfully. "I bet he's hot."

"You make that bet on every guy," I tease, piling my makeup into a bag.

She grins, but there's sadness in her eyes. "Yeah, you're probably right." She sighs. "Will I at least get to see this mysterious Micha—who you've refused to speak about our whole eight months of sharing a dorm together—when I drop you off at your house?"

"I hope not," I mutter and her face sinks. "I'm sorry, but Micha and I...we didn't leave on a good note and I haven't talked to him since I left for school in August." Micha doesn't even know where I am.

She heaves an overly stuffed pink duffle bag over her shoulder. "That sounds like a perfect story for our twelve hour road trip back home."

"Back home..." My eyes widen at the empty room that's been my home for the last eight months. I'm not ready to go back home and face everyone I bailed on. Especially Micha. He can see through me better than a mirror.

"Are you okay?" Lila asks with concern.

My lips bend upward into a stiff smile as I stuff my panicked feeling in a box hidden deep inside my heart. "I'm great. Let's go."

We head out the door, with the last of our boxes in our hands. I pat my empty pockets, realizing I forgot my phone.

"Hold on. I think I forgot my phone." Setting my box on the ground, I run back to the room and glance around at the garbage bag, a few empty plastic cups on the bed, and the mirror. "Where is it?" I check under the bed and in the closet.

The soft tune of Pink's "Funhouse" sings underneath the trash bag—my unknown ID ringtone. I pick up the bag and there is my phone with the screen lit up. I scoop it up and my heart stops. It's not an unknown number, just one that was never programmed into my phone when I switched carriers.

"Micha." My hands tremble, unable to answer, yet powerless to silence it.

"Aren't you going to answer that?" Lila enters the room, her face twisted in confusion. "What's up? You look like you just saw a ghost or something."

The phone stops ringing and I tuck it into the back pocket of my shorts. "We should get going. We have a long trip ahead of us."

Lila salutes me. "Yes, ma'am."

She links arms with me and we head out to the parking lot. When we reach the car, my phone beeps.

Voicemail.

## Micha

"Why is Ella Daniels such a common name," Ethan grunts from the computer chair. His legs are kicked up on the desk as he lazily scrolls the internet. "The list is freaking endless, man. I can't even see straight anymore." He rubs his eyes. "Can I take a break?"

Shaking my head, I pace my room with the phone to my ear, kicking the clothes and other shit on my floor out of the way. I'm on hold with the main office at Indiana University, waiting for answers that probably aren't there. But I have to try—I've been trying ever since the day Ella vanished from my life. The day I promised myself that I'd find her no matter what.

"Are you sure her dad doesn't know where she is?" Ethan flops his head back against the headrest of the office chair. "I swear that old man knows more than he's letting on."

"If he does, he's not telling me," I say. "Or his trashed mind has misplaced the information."

Ethan swivels the chair around. "Have you ever considered that maybe she doesn't want to be found?"

"Every single day," I mutter. "Which makes me even more determined to find her."

Ethan refocuses his attention to the computer and continues his search through the endless amount of Ella Daniels in the country. But I'm not even sure if she's still in the country.

The secretary returns to the phone and gives me the answer I was expecting. This isn't the Ella Daniels I'm looking for.

I hang up and throw my phone onto the bed. "God Dammit!"

Ethan glances over his shoulder. "No luck?"

I sink down on my bed and let my head fall into my hands. "It was another dead end."

"Look, I know you miss her and everything," he says, typing on the keyboard. "But you need to get your crap together. All this whining is giving me a headache."

He's right. I shake my pity party off, slip on a black hoodie, and a pair of black boots. "I've got to go down to the shop to pick up a part. You staying or going?"

He drops his feet to the floor and gratefully shoves away from the desk. "Yeah, but can we stop by my house. I need to pick up my drums for tonight's practice. Are you going to that or are you still on strike?"

Pulling my hood over my head, I head for the door. "Nah, I got some stuff to do tonight."

"That's bull." He reaches to shut off the computer screen. "Everyone knows the only reason you don't play anymore is because of Ella. But you need to quit being a pussy and get over her."

"I think I'm going to…" I smack his hand away from the off button and squint at a picture of a girl on the screen. She has the same dark green eyes and long auburn hair as Ella. But she has on a dress and there isn't any heavy black liner around her eyes. She also looks fake, like she's pretending to be happy. The Ella I knew never pretended.

But it has to be her.

"Dude, what are you doing?" Ethan complains as I snatch my phone off my bed. "I thought we were giving up for the day."

I tap the screen and call information. "Yeah, can I get a number for Ella Daniels in Las Vegas, Nevada." I wait, worried she's not going to be listed.

"She's been down in *Vegas*." Ethan peers at the photo on the screen of Ella standing next to a girl with blonde hair and blue eyes in front of the UNLV campus. "She looks weird, but kinda hot. So is the girl she's with."

"Yeah, but she's not your type."

"Everyone's my type. Besides, she could be a stripper and that's definitely my type."

The operator comes back on and she gives me a few numbers listed, one of the numbers belongs to a girl living on the campus. I dial that number and walk out into the hall to get some privacy. It rings and rings and rings and then Ella's voice comes on the voicemail. She still sounds the same, only a little unemotional, like she's pretending to be happy, but can't quite get there.

When it beeps, I take a deep breath and pour my heart out to the voicemail.

Read more about Nova & Quinton's story.

See the next page for a preview of

# *Breaking Nova.*

# Chapter 1

*Fifteen months later…*
*May 19, Day 1 of Summer Break*

## Nova

I have the web camera set up perfectly angled straight at my face. The green light on the screen is flickering insanely, like it can't wait for me to start recording. But I'm not sure what I'll say or what the point of all this is, other than my film professor suggested it.

He'd actually suggested to the entire class—and probably all of his classes—telling us that if we really wanted to get into filming, we should practice over the summer, even if we weren't enrolled in any summer classes. He said, "A true videographer loves looking at the world through an alternative eye, and he loves to record how he sees things in a different light." He was quoting straight out of a textbook, like most of my professors do, but for some reason something about what he said struck a nerve.

Maybe it was because of the video Landon made right before

the last seconds of his life. I've never actually watched his video, though. I never really wanted to and I can't, anyway. I'm too afraid of what I'll see or what I won't see. Or maybe it's because seeing him like that means finally accepting that he's gone. Forever.

I originally signed up for the film class because I waited too long to enroll for classes and I needed one more elective. I'm a general major and don't really have a determined interest path, and the only classes that weren't full were Intro to Video Design or Intro to Theater. At least with the video class I'd be behind a lens instead of standing up in front of everyone where they could strip me down and evaluate me. With video, I get to do the evaluating. Turns out, though, that I liked the class, and I found out that there's something fascinating about seeing the world through a lens, like I could be looking at it from anyone's point of view and maybe see things at a different angle, like Landon did during his last few moments alive. So I decided that I would try to make some videos this summer, to get some insight on myself, Landon, and maybe life.

I turn on "Jesus Christ" by Brand New and let it play in the background. I shove the stack of psychology books off the computer chair and onto the floor, clearing off a place for me to sit. I've been collecting the books for the last year, trying to learn about the human psyche—Landon's psyche—but books hold just words on pages, not thoughts in *his* head.

I sit down on the swivel chair and clear my throat. I have no makeup on. The sun is descending behind the mountains, but I refuse to turn the bedroom light on. Without the light the screen is dark, and I look like a shadow on a backdrop. But it's perfect. Just how I want it. I tap the cursor and the green light shifts to red. I open my mouth, ready to speak, but then I freeze up. I've never been one for being on camera or in pictures. I'd liked being behind the scenes, and now I'm purposely throwing myself into the spotlight.

"People say that time heals all wounds, and maybe they're right." I keep my eyes on the computer screen, watching my lips move. "But what if the wounds don't heal correctly, like when cuts leave behind nasty scars, or when broken bones mend together, but aren't as smooth anymore?" I glance at my arm, my brows furrowing as I touch the scar along the uneven section of skin with my fingertip. "Does it mean they're really healed? Or is that the body did what it could to fix what broke..." I trail off, counting backward from ten, gathering my thoughts. "But what exactly broke...with me...with him...I'm not sure, but it feels like I need to find out...somehow...about him...about myself...but how the fuck do I find out about him when the only person that truly knew what was real is...gone?" I blink and then click the screen off, and it goes black.

\* \* \*

*May 27, Day 7 of Summer Break*

I started this ritual when I got to college. I wake up and count the seconds it takes for the sun to rise over the hill. It's my way of preparing for another day I don't want to prepare for, knowing that it's another day to add to my list of days I've lived without Landon.

This morning worked a little differently, though. I'm home for my first summer break of college, and instead of the hills that surround Idaho, the sun advances over the immense Wyoming mountains that enclose Maple Grove, the small town I grew up in. The change makes it difficult to get out of bed, because it's unfamiliar and breaks the routine I set up over the last eight months. And that routine was what kept me intact. Before it, I was a mess, unstable, out of control. I had no control. And I need control, otherwise I end up on the bathroom floor with a razor in my hand with the need to understand why he did it—what pushed him to that point. But the only way to do that is to make my veins run dry, and it turned out that I didn't have it in me. I was too weak, or maybe it was too strong. I honestly don't know anymore, what's considered weak and what's considered strong. What's right and what's wrong. Who I was and who I should be.

I've been home for a week, and my mom and stepfather are watching me like hawks, like they expect me to break down again, after almost a year. But I'm in control now. *In control.*

After I get out of bed and take a shower, I sit for exactly five minutes in front of my computer, staring at the file folder that holds the video clip Landon made before he died. I always give myself five minutes to look at it, not because I'm planning on opening it, but because it recorded his last few minutes, captured him, his thoughts, his words, his face. It feels like the last piece of him that I have left. I wonder if one day, somehow, I'll finally be able to open it. But at this moment, in the state of mind I'm stuck in, it just doesn't seem possible. Not much does.

Once the five minutes are over, I put on my swimsuit, then pull on a floral sundress over it and strap some leather bands onto my wrists. Then I pull the curtains shut, so Landon's house will be out of sight and out of mind, before heading back to my computer desk to record a short clip.

I click Record and stare at the screen as I take a few collected breaths. "So I was thinking about my last recording—my first— and I was trying to figure out what the point of this is—or if there even had to be a point. " I rest my arms on the desk and lean closer to the screen, assessing my blue eyes. "I guess if there is a point, it would be for me to discover something. About myself or maybe about…him, because it feels like there's still so much stuff I'm missing…so many unanswered questions and all the lack of answers leaves me feeling lost, not just about why the hell he did it, but about what kind of person I am that he could leave so easily…Who was I then? Who am I now? I really don't know…But maybe when I look back and watch these one day far, far down the road, I'll realize what I really think about life and I'll finally get some answers to what leaves me confused every single day, because right now I'm about as lost as a damn bottle floating in gross, murky water."

I pause, contemplating as I tap my fingers on the desk. "Or maybe I'll be able to backtrack through my thoughts and figure out why he did it." I inhale and then exhale loudly as my pulse begins to thrash. "And if you're not me and you're watching these, then you're probably wondering who *he* is, but I'm not sure if I'm ready to say his name yet. Hopefully I'll get there. One day—someday, but who knows…maybe I'll always be as clueless and as lost as I am now."

I leave it at that and turn the computer off, wondering how long I'm going to continue this pointless charade, this time filler, because right now that's how it feels. I shove the chair away and head out of my room. It takes fifteen steps to reach the end of the hall, then another ten to get me to the table. They're each taken at a consistent pace and with even lengths. If I were filming right now, my steps would be smooth and perfect, steady as a rock.

"Good morning, my beautiful girl," my mother singsongs as she whisks around the kitchen, moving from the stove to the fridge, then to the cupboard. She's making cookies, and the air smells like cinnamon and nutmeg, and it reminds me of my childhood when my dad and I would sit at the table, waiting to stuff our mouths with sugar. But he's not here anymore and instead Daniel, my stepfather, is sitting at the table. He's not waiting for the cookies. In fact he hates sugar and loves healthy food, mostly eating stuff that looks like rabbit food.

"Good morning, Nova. It's so good to have you back." He has on a suit and tie, and he's drinking grapefruit juice and eating dry toast. They've been married for three years, and he's not a bad guy. He's always taken care of my mom and me, but he's very plain, orderly, and somewhat boring. He could never replace my dad's spontaneous, adventurous, down-to-earth personality.

I plop down in the chair and rest my arms on the kitchen table. "Good morning."

My mom takes a bowl out of the cupboard and turns to me with a worried look on her face. "Nova, sweetie, I want to make sure you're okay…with being home. We can get you into therapy here, if you need it, and you're still taking your medication, right?"

"Yes mom, I'm still taking my medication," I reply with a sigh and lower my head onto my arms and shut my eyes. I've been on antianxiety medication for a while now. I'm not sure if it really does anything or not, but the therapist prescribed it to me so I take it. "I take them every morning, but I stopped going to therapy back in December, because it doesn't do anything but waste time." Because no matter that, they always want me to talk about what I saw that morning—what I did and why I did it—and I can't even think about it, let only talk about it.

"Yeah, I know, honey, but things are different when you're here," she says quietly.

I remember the hell I put her through before I left. The lack of sleep, the crying…cutting my wrist open. But that's in the past now. I don't cry as much, and my wrist has healed.

"I'm fine, Mom." I open my eyes, sit back up, and overlap my fingers in front of me. "So please, pretty please, with a cherry on top and icing and candy corn, would you please stop asking?"

"You sound just like your father…everything had to be referenced to sugar," she remarks with a frown as she sets the bowl down on the counter. In a lot of ways she looks like me: long brown hair, a thin frame, and a sprinkle of freckles on her nose. But her blue eyes are a lot brighter than mine, to the point where they almost sparkle. "Honey, I know you keep saying that you're fine, but you look so sad…and I know you were doing okay at school, but you're back here now, and everything that happened is right across the street." She opens a drawer and selects a large wooden spoon, before bumping the drawer shut with her hip. "I just don't want the memories to get to you now that you're home and so close to…everything."

I stare at my reflection in the stainless-steel microwave. It's not the clearest. In fact, my face looks a little distorted and warped, like I'm looking into a funhouse mirror, my own face nearly a stranger. But if I tilt sideways just a little, I almost look normal, like my old self. "I'm fine," I repeat, observing how blank my expression looks when I say it. "Memories are just memories." Really, it doesn't matter what they are, because I can't see the parts that I know will rip my heart back open: the last few steps leading up to Landon's finality and the soundless moments afterward, before I cracked apart. I worked hard to stitch my heart back up after it was torn open, even if I hadn't done it neatly.

"Nova." She sighs as she starts mixing the cookie batter. "You can't just try to forget without dealing with it first. It's unhealthy."

"Forgetting *is* dealing with it." I grab an apple from a basket on the table, no longer wanting to talk about it because it's in the past, where it belongs.

"Nova, honey," she says sadly. She's always tried to get me to talk about that day. But what she doesn't get is that I can't remember, even if I really tried, which I never will. It's like my brain's developed it's own brain and it won't allow those thoughts out, because once they're out, they're real. And I don't want them to be real—I don't want to remember *him* like that. Or me.

I push up from the chair, cutting her off. "I think I'm going to hang out next to the pool today, and Delilah will probably be over in a bit."

"If that's what you want." My mom smiles halfheartedly at me, wanting to say more, but fearing what it'll do to me. I don't blame her, either. She's the one who found me on the bathroom floor, but she thinks it's more than it was. I was just trying to find out what he felt like—what was going on inside of him when he decided to go through with it.

I nod, grab a can of soda out of the fridge, and give her a hug before I head for the sliding glass door. "That's what I want."

She swallows hard, looking like she might cry because she thinks she's lost her daughter. "Well, if you need me, I'm here." She turns back to her bowl.

She's been saying that to me since I was thirteen, ever since I watched my dad die. I've never taken her up on the offer, even though we've always had a good relationship. Talking about death with her—at all—doesn't work for me. At this point in my life, I couldn't talk to her about it even if I wanted to. I have my silence now, which is my healing, my escape, my sanctuary. Without it, I'd hear the noises of that morning, see the bleeding images, and feel the crushing pain connected to them. If I saw them, then I'd finally have to accept that Landon's gone.

\* \* \*

I don't like unknown places. They make me anxious and I have trouble thinking—breathing. One of the therapists I first saw diagnosed me with obsessive-compulsive disorder. I'm not sure if he was right, though, because he moved out of town not too long after. I was left with a therapist in training, so to speak, and he decided that I was just depressed and had anxiety, hence the anti-anxiety medication for the last year and three months.

The unfamiliarity of the backyard disrupts my counting, and it takes me forever to get to the pool. By the time I arrive at the lawn chair, I know how many steps it took me to get here, how many seconds it took me to sit down, and how many more seconds it took for Delilah to arrive and then take a seat beside me. I know how many rocks are on the path leading to the porch—twenty-two—how many branches are on the tree shielding the sunlight from us—seventy-eight. The only thing I don't know is how many seconds, hours, years, decades, it will take before I can let go of the goddamn self-induced numbness. Until then I'll count, focus on numbers instead of the feelings always floating inside me, the ones linked to images immersed just beneath the surface.

Delilah and I lie in lawn chairs in the middle of my backyard with the pool behind us and the sun bearing down on us as we tan in our swimsuits. She's been my best friend for the past year or so. Our sudden friendship was strange, because we'd gone to high school together but never really talked. She and I were in different social circles and I had Landon. But after it happened… after he died…I had no one, and the last few weeks of high school were torture. Then I met her, and she was nice and she didn't look at me like I was about to shatter. We hit it off, and honestly, I have no idea what I'd do without her now. She's been there for me, she shows me how to have fun, and she reminds me that life still exists in the world, even if it's brief.

"Good God, has it always been this hot here?" Delilah fans her face with her hand as she yawns. "I remember it being colder."

"I think so." I pick up a cup of iced tea on the table between us and prop up on my elbow to take a sip. "We could go in," I suggest, setting my glass down. I turn it in a circle until it's perfectly in place on the condensation ring it left behind, and then I wipe the moisture from my lips with the back of my hand and rest my head back against the chair. "We do have air-conditioning."

Delilah laughs sardonically as she reaches for the sparkly pink flask in her bag. "Yeah, right. Are you kidding me?" She pauses, examining her fiery red nails, then unscrews the lid off the flask. "No offense. I didn't mean for that to sound rude, but your mom and dad are a little overwhelming." She takes a swig from the flask and holds it out in my direction.

"Stepdad," I correct absentmindedly. I wrap my lips around the top of the flask and take a tiny swallow, then hand it back to her and close my eyes. "And they're just lonely. I'm the only child and I've been gone for almost a year."

She laughs again, but it's breezier than before. "They're seriously the most overbearing parents I know. They call you every day at school and text you a thousand times." She puts the flask back into her bag.

"They just worry about me." They didn't use to. My mom was really carefree before my dad died, and then she got concerned about how his death and seeing it affected me. Then Landon died, and now all she does is constantly worry.

"*I* worry about you, too," Delilah mumbles. She waits for me to say something, but I don't—I can't. Delilah knows about what happened with Landon, but we never *really* talk about what I saw. And that's one of the things I like about her—that she doesn't ask questions.

*One...two...three...four...five...breathe...six...seven... eight...breathe...* Balling my hands into fists, I fight to calm myself down, but the darkness is ascending inside me, and it will take me over if I let it and drag me down into the memory I won't remember; my last memory of Landon.

"I have a brilliant idea," she interrupts my counting. "We could go check out Dylan and Tristan's new place."

My eyes open and I slant my head to the side. My hands are on my stomach, and I can feel my pulse beating through my fingertips, inconsistent. Tracking the beats is difficult, but I try anyway. "You want to go see your ex-boyfriend's place. *Seriously?*"

Swinging her legs over the edge of the chair, Delilah sits up and slips her sunglasses up to the top of her head. "What? I'm totally curious what he ended up like." She presses her fingertips to the corners of her eyes, plucking out gobs of kohl eyeliner.

"Yeah, but isn't it kind of weird to show up randomly after not talking to him in like forever, especially after how bad your guys' breakup was," I say. "I mean, if Tristan hadn't stepped in, you would have probably hit Dylan."

"Yeah, probably, but that's all in the past." She chews on her thumbnail and gives me a guilt-ridden look as she smears the tanning-spray grease off her bare stomach. "Besides that's not technically accurate. We kind of talked yesterday."

Frowning, I sit up and refasten the elastic around my long, wavy brown hair, securing it in a ponytail. "Are you serious?" I ask, and when she doesn't respond, I add, "Nine months ago, when he cheated on you, you swore up and down that you'd never talk to that"—I make air quotes—"'fucking, lying, cheating bastard' again. In fact, if I remember right, it was the main reason you decided to go to college with me—because you needed a break."

"Did I say that really?" She feigns forgetfulness as she taps her finger on her chin. "Well, like everything else in my life, I've decided to have a change of heart." She reaches for the tanning spray on the table between us. "And besides, I did need a break, not just from him, but from my mom and this town, but now we're back and I figure I might as well have some fun while I'm here. College wore me out."

Delilah is the most indecisive person I've ever met. During our freshman year, she changed majors three times, dyed her hair from red, to black, then back to red again, and went through about a half a dozen boyfriends. I secretly love it, despite how much I pretend that I don't. It was what kind of drew me to her; her uncaring, nonchalant attitude, and the way she could forget things in the snap of a finger. I wish I could be the same way sometimes, and if I hang around her a lot, there are a few moments when I can get my mind on the same carefree level as hers.

"What have you two been talking about?" I wonder, plucking a piece of grass off my leg. "And please don't tell me it's getting back together, because I don't want to see you get crushed like that again."

Her smile shines as she tucks strands of her red hair behind her heavily studded ears, then she removes the lid from the tanning spray. "What is with you and Dylan? He's always put you on edge."

"Because he's sketchy. *And* he cheated on you."

"He's not sketchy…he's mysterious. And he was drunk when he cheated."

"Delilah, you deserve better than that."

She narrows her eyes at me as she spritzes her legs with tanning spray. "I'm not better than him, Nova. I've done supercrappy things, hurt people. I've made mistakes—we all have."

I stab my nails into the palms of my hands, thinking of all the mistakes I made and their consequences. "Yes, you are better. All he's ever done is cheat on you and deal drugs."

She slaps her hand on her knee. "Hey, he doesn't deal anymore. He stopped dealing a year ago." She clicks the cap back onto the tanning spray and tosses it into her bag.

I sigh, push my sunglasses up over my head, and massage my temples. "So what has he been up to for a year?" I lower my hands and blink against the sunlight.

She shrugs, and then her lips expand to a grin as she grabs my hand and stands, tugging me to my feet. "How about we go change out of our swimsuits, head over to his place, and find out?" When I open my mouth to protest, she adds, "It'd be a good distraction for the day."

"I'm not really looking for a distraction, though."

"Well, then you could go over and see Tristan." She bites back an amused smirk. "Maybe reheat things."

I glare at her. "We hooked up one time and that's because I was drunk and…" *Vulnerable.* I'd actually been really drunk, and my thoughts had been all over the place because of an unexpected visit from Landon's parents that morning. They'd wanted to give me some of his sketchings, which they'd found in a trunk upstairs—sketchings of me. I'd barely been able to take them without crying, and then I'd run off, looking to get drunk and forget about the drawings, Landon, and the pain of him leaving. Tristan, Dylan's best friend—and roommate—was the first guy I came across after way, way too many Coronas and shots. I started making out with him without even saying hello.

He was the first guy I'd made out with since Landon, and I spent the entire night afterward crying and rocking on the bathroom floor, counting the cracks in the tile and trying to get myself to calm down and stop feeling guilty for kissing someone else, because Landon was gone and he took a part of me with him—at least that was what it feels like. What's left of me is a hollow shell full of denial and tangled with confusion. I have no idea who I am anymore. I really don't. And I'm not sure if I want to know or not.

"Oh come on, Nova." She releases my hand and claps her hands in front of her. "Please, can we just go and try to have some fun?"

I sigh, defeated, and nod, knowing that the true feelings of why I don't want to go over there lie more in the fact that I hate new places than anything else. Unfamiliar situations put me on edge, because I hate the unknown. It reminds me just how much the unknown controls everything, and my counting can sometimes get a little out of hand. But I don't want to argue anymore with Delilah, either, because then my anxiety will get me worked up and the counting will, too. Either way, I know I'm going to have a head full of numbers. At least if I go with Delilah, then I can keep an eye on her and maybe she'll end up happy. And really, that's all I can ask for. For everyone to be happy. But as I all too painfully know, you can't force someone to be happy, no matter how much you wish you could.

# You Might Also Like...

**FOREVER**

## Looking for more great reads?
## We've got you covered.

*Sometimes life takes you off course...*

## *THE EDGE OF NEVER*

Twenty-year-old Camryn Bennett thought she knew exactly where her life was going. But after a wild night at the hottest club in downtown Raleigh, North Carolina, she shocks everyone—including herself—when she decides to leave the only life she's ever known and set out on her own. Grabbing her purse and her cell phone, Camryn boards a Greyhound bus ready to find herself. Instead, she finds Andrew Parrish.

Sexy and exciting, Andrew lives life like there is no tomorrow. He persuades Camryn to do things she never thought she would and shows her how to give in to her deepest, most forbidden desires. Soon he becomes the center of her daring new life, pulling love and lust and emotion out of her in ways she never imagined possible. But there is more to Andrew than Camryn realizes. Will his secret push them together—or destroy them forever?

Five months ago, Camryn and Andrew, both dealing with personal hardships, met on a Greyhound bus. They fell in love and proved that when two people are meant to be together, fate will find a way to make it happen.

Now, in the highly anticipated sequel to *The Edge of Never*, Camryn and Andrew are pursuing their love for music and living life to the fullest as they always swore to do. But when tragedy befalls them, their relationship is put to the ultimate test. As Camryn tries to numb her pain, Andrew makes a bold decision: to get their life back on track, they'll set out on another cross-country road trip. Together they find excitement, passion, adventure, and challenges they never could have anticipated.

New York Times *best-selling author J. A. Redmerski brings us a stunning and heart-wrenching new novel about a couple who find each other in their darkest moment.*

Since they were kids, Elias Kline and Brayelle Bates have been inseparable. When Bray moves to South Carolina, separating the two for the first time, they both at last realize that their innocent childhood friendship has developed into something much more. So when Bray finally returns to Georgia—and to Elias—things between them couldn't be more perfect... until one fateful night changes everything.

Desperate not to go to prison for a terrible accident, Elias and Bray decide to run. As they try to make the most of their freedom, the two find themselves relying on a rebellious group of people who tempt the duo into a wild and daring new life. But they can't run from their troubles forever.

As the consequences of their past catch up to them, the couple must face reality. Even if they can make it through the unimaginable, Elias knows the truth about Bray's painful history, and in the end he may not be able to save Bray from herself...

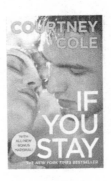

*In the best-selling tradition of*
*J.A. Redmerski, Jessica Sorensen,*
*S.C. Stephens, and Jamie McGuire...*

## IF YOU STAY

Twenty-four-year-old Pax Tate is an asshole. Seriously. He's a tattooed, rock-hard bad boy with a tough attitude to match. His mother died when Pax was seven, leaving a hole in his heart filled with an intense guilt that he doesn't understand. What he does know is that he and his dad were left alone, and they have never been close. Now, he uses drugs and women to cope with the black void in his soul. He pretends that the emptiness isn't there and this has always worked... until he meets Mila.

Sweet, beautiful Mila Hill is the fresh air that Pax has never known in his life. He doesn't know how to not hurt her, but he quickly realizes that he'd better figure it out because he needs her to breathe. When the memories of his mother's death resurface to haunt Pax, Mila is there to save him from his overwhelming guilt. Mila restores his broken heart, even as she evokes his powerful, sexual desires. Now for Pax to keep Mila, he needs to work on his issues and stop being an asshole. But is that enough to make her stay?

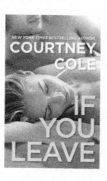

## IF YOU LEAVE

Twenty-six-year old Gabriel Vincent is a badass hero. Or he used to be, anyway. As an ex-Army Ranger, Gabe never thought he needed anyone. But after one horrible night in Afghanistan scars him in a way that he can't get past, he needs someone who can help him heal... even if he doesn't realize it.

Twenty-five-year old Madison Hill doesn't need anybody... or so she thinks. She grew up watching her parents' messed-up abusive relationship and she knows there's no way in hell that she's ever letting that happen to her.

They don't know it in the beginning, but Gabriel and Madison will soon develop a weakness: each other.

But Gabriel's got a secret, a hidden monster that he's afraid Maddy could never overcome... And Maddy's got issues she's afraid Gabe will never understand. They quickly realize that they need each other to be whole, but at the same time they know that they've got demons to fight.

And the problem with demons is that they never die quietly.

*Sometimes before we fall... we fly.*

One dark moment was all it took to turn twenty-four-year-old Dominic Kinkaide's world black. On the night of his high school graduation, a single incident changed him forever, and he became a hardened man—famous in the eyes of the world, but tortured inside. Now all he cares about is losing himself in the roles that he plays.

At twenty-three years old, Jacey Vincent doesn't realize how much her father's indifference has affected her. She is proof that sometimes it isn't one specific moment that wrecks a person, but an absence of moments. She tries to find acceptance in the arms of men to fill the void—a plan that has worked just fine for her, until she meets Dominic.

When jaded Dominic and strong-willed Jacey are thrown together, the combination of his secrets and her issues turns their attraction into the perfect storm. It could change their lives for good—if it doesn't tear them both apart...

College student Pixie Marshall wants her life to go back to normal, but the jagged scar on her chest is a constant reminder of hurt and loss. It's not nearly as painful as the scar Levi Andrews left on her heart, though. Once he was her best friend and possibly—hopefully—more. But when she needed him most, he abandoned her. Now, the one person she's vowed to forget will be working with her all summer at Willow Inn.

Now that they're sharing living space, Levi can't avoid Pixie anymore. Maybe it will be okay, as long as he stops looking into her gorgeous green eyes. Eyes that know what's inside him: the guilt, the shame, the unspeakable things. Every instinct he has screams to touch her, to protect her, to wrap her in his arms and kiss away her pain. But after everything they've been through, can he allow himself to love her again?

Daren Ackwood is a bad boy with a mysterious past. He's the kind of guy who knows he can get any girl he wants. Kayla doesn't do bad boys-in any sense of the word. They have a tendency to leave scars and dust trails in their wake, and Kayla isn't running short on either. So when Daren rolls up to her father's funeral in his shiny sports car, Kayla knows she needs to keep her distance during her brief stay in this tiny God-forsaken town. She's here to take care of her father's will, nothing more. The trouble is, Daren doesn't see it that way. And he usually gets his way.

Jenna's grandmother is dying. That's nothing new. The old woman has been "dying" for over a decade. And people say Jenna is the drama queen in the family. Nevertheless, Jenna's agreed to make the trip to New Orleans and say her farewells. But when her friend Jack invites himself along for the ride—sexy, infuriating Jack—Jenna realizes there's a good chance she might die before her feisty grandmother.

Sure, Jack needs a ride to LSU. And sure, he likes driving Jenna insane with questions about her future. But the idea of his beautiful friend trekking across the country by herself actually worries him. So he called "shotgun" and designated himself bodyguard. But after a few hot nights on the road and too much exposure to Jenna's wild side, Jack's pretty sure the only body that needs guarding on this trip is his.

# About the Author

The *New York Times* and *USA Today* bestselling author, Jessica Sorensen, lives with her husband and three kids. When she's not writing, she spends her time reading and hanging out with her family.

Learn more at:

jessicasorensen.com

@jessFallenStar

Facebook.com /pages/Jessica-Sorensen/165335743524509

CPSIA information can be obtained at www.ICGtesting.com
Printed in the USA
BVOW08s2014060515

399238BV00001B/11/P